WHAT READERS SAY

Stories for all ages

These books are amazing! I couldn't put them down. The characters are so real, I felt like I was living with them. I love how courageous Rose is.

～ *Eva Richter, 12 years old*

I loved the books so much. It took me several days to finish "A Silver Moon for Rose" because I just didn't want the story to end.

～ *Rose Rose, 74 years old, retired teacher*

Comments on earlier books in the series

Carefully researched and lovingly written.

～ *Amy Hill Hearth, author of "Having Our Say"*

Enthralling – touching, wrenching, joyous, irresistible. A treasured journey.

～ *Gene Shalit, NBC TV*

More than a century has passed since Rose Hibbard had to deal with problems of a parent's alcoholism and an indifferent adult world – but they are not so different from the problems some teenagers face today. Ruth Bass has written a book memorable for its insights and its understanding of the hearts and minds of young women and the challenges they face – no matter what century they live in.

～ *Michelle Gillett, poet, Berkshire Eagle review*

Sarah Meets Silas

Sarah Meets Silas

by Ruth Bass
A Prequel to Sarah's Daughter

Also by Ruth Bass

Sarah's Daughter

Rose

A Silver Moon for Rose

Fresh from the Garden Cookbooks (8)

Sarah Meets Silas is a work of fiction.
Names, characters, places and incidents are the products of the author's imagination or are used fictitiously. Any resemblance to actual events, locales, or persons, living or dead, is entirely coincidental.

Copyright © 2021 by Ruth Bass
All rights reserved. No part of this book may be used or reproduced in any form, electronic or mechanical, including photocopying, recording, or scanning into any information storage and retrieval system, without written permission from the author except in the case of brief quotation embodied in critical articles and reviews.

Printed in the United States of America

The Troy Book Makers • Troy, New York • thetroybookmakers.com

ISBN: 978-1-61468-688-0

For Tracer,

The best of caretakers

Sarah Meets Silas

CHAPTER ONE

Sarah spent more than an hour in the big barn where quilts and vegetables were displayed. The garden at her house had vegetables at least as nice as these, she thought, but she did admire the quilts, especially the ones with tiny embroidery stitches around appliquéd flowers. She paid ten cents for a small drawing of a quilt block she particularly liked, and she bought two quilting needles for twenty cents from her share of the egg money. She wished for a moment that she'd saved a little for a tumbler of lemonade. It was so hot. She worried the back of her shirtwaist might be showing damp.

She moved outside, where a slight breeze worked at pushing the heat away and decided to watch the men and boys try their hand at the various games. One of her favorites was the high striker, and she nearly laughed out loud when she saw Corey Leonard take his place with the mallet. Surely the blacksmith's muscles would send the chunk of coal to the top, and the cowbell would ring.

Corey didn't disappoint. The coal flew upward, the bell clanged, and the men waiting in line cheered. She saw Corey head toward the man in charge to get his prize and noticed that the man wasn't pleased when Corey also asked for another ticket and took his place at the end of the line. She decided to stay and see if anyone else had good luck.

But three men and two high school boys failed before it was Corey's turn again. The ticket man said, "Hold it. Wanna try harder?" Corey nodded, the man adjusted something near the lever at the base of the tower, and Sarah held her breath as the mallet rose over the blacksmith's head.

Clang! Corey grinned, the ticket man shook his hand and readjusted the lever for more ordinary customers. With two small dolls under his arm, Corey moved off to another game. Sarah strolled on, too, pausing by a booth where men were shooting arrows at crude drawings of deer and pheasants tacked to a wall. She stopped at a game where a farmer had cut a ragged hole in a large piece of deer hide and stretched it between two poles. Young men were putting down their change for baseballs, and she realized they were hurling them at a face that had appeared in the hole and vanished when the ball came.

She was startled to see that the face was black, belonging to a small Negro boy who was far too quick for any of the young men. Even as she wondered where a Negro boy had come from, she watched him win every time. Sometimes the boy didn't even move because he gauged where the ball would go and grinned as it whacked the deer hide. And then a tall young man presented his money, accepted the two baseballs allowed and stepped up to the throw line. His right hand came up, the ball sped toward the target and hit wide of the mark. The boy's eyes slid sideways, judging the track of the ball, and he didn't move, his grin wide. The young man almost instantly fired his second ball with his left hand. With a sickening thud, the ball hit the boy on the nose, and he fell out of sight, but not before a scream cut the air, and Sarah saw blood streaming from his mouth and nose.

She yelped, started toward the man taking tickets at this game and then stopped. What could she do? She looked back at the young man. He and his friends were laughing in triumph as he grabbed his stuffed animal prize from the shelf near the canvas. She felt suddenly ill and turned away, embarrassed to find tears streaming down her face. She felt she might have seen that young man before, but couldn't place him. He had tricked the little boy and hurt him badly. She moved farther away, trying to choke down the sobs that were pushing their way up her throat. She slipped into the field behind the row of booths and let the sobs come. At least she was alone here, and no one would hear her. Where, she thought, had a little black boy come from anyway. This county had no Negro families that she knew of.

After a few minutes, her sobs subsided and she sat down on a rock, her basket beside her, her head in her hands. She'd like to find that baseball pitcher and give him a piece of her mind, but first she'd have to figure out how to cover up the fact that her face must look awful.

"Need a handkerchief?" a voice said behind her. "Sorry, didn't mean to startle you," the voice added as Sarah jumped to her feet.

She turned and saw a young man about her age, his hand outstretched with what appeared to be a clean handkerchief. She took it and dabbed at her face, then blew her nose, thinking how rude and loud that sounded, and wondering at the same time how she could be so vain when that boy was bleeding and hurting.

"He's going to be all right," the handkerchief person said carefully, his eyes on her face.

"How do you know?" Sarah said, tears welling up again and threatening to spill over.

"Went back to see. His boss said he'd been hit once or twice before, and it was more blood than damage. Didn't lose a tooth. The lemonade people didn't want to give up any ice, but talk about blood persuaded 'em."

Suddenly feeling weak in the knees, Sarah sat down again. She'd never liked the sight of blood, from human or animal, and she'd always had to steel herself not to faint. Actually, when one of the haying crew had cut his hand on the mower blades, she'd managed to bandage him up and had then gone into the privy and thrown up everything she'd eaten that day and then some. Her mother had remarked that it was quite acceptable to collapse once the emergency was over, and Sarah had treasured that idea for a good while.

"You right now?" the young man persisted, sounding calm but not really looking at her. Sarah wished he'd just go away and let her be, let her dry her face and settle her stomach. At the same time, she found herself wanting him to stay. Even in her present state she was aware of how good looking he was and how kind he seemed to be. Hard working, she reckoned, judging from the calloused hand that had proffered the handkerchief. She sighed and nodded.

"I could sit a minute until you're steady," the young man said. "Name's Silas Hibbard. Figure if you've borrowed my hanky, we'd better be introduced."

"Sarah Sherman," she answered, a smile trembling its way to the corners of her mouth. "My mother would say we should not have spoken until introduced, but sometimes her rules don't work perfectly. I thank you for your attention – and your hanky."

"You may return it now if you've done with it," Silas said, thinking fast about how he could find out where this curious young lady lived. "Or perhaps you'd launder it for me and return it another time." He moved toward her and perched on the edge of a rock facing her.

Sarah stared at him in astonishment. Forward, her mother would say, very forward. But in a nice way, her brain countered. She didn't want him to go, didn't want him to stay, wanted to see him again when she wasn't sobbing, wished he'd stop looking at her like that.

"My mother," she started, "my mother would say I am obligated to wash and iron your handkerchief." And then, her mischievous side emerging, she added with a small smile, "Providing you have another at home."

"Yes, ma'am," he answered quickly. "Washed and ironed. By my mother. Sometimes by my sister Minnie, but she leaves wrinkles."

They sat and looked at each other, each wondering how to take the next step. Except for square dances, where she was as likely as not to be partnered with a ninety-year-old rather than one of the boys, Sarah had little experience with social occasions. And her mother had not provided any inkling about how to deal with a random stranger who loaned his handkerchief. She'd merely instructed her not to speak with strangers, especially of the male sort, and here she was, offering to do his laundry.

"Where is he from?" Sarah asked suddenly.

"Ripton Academy. He's a pitcher. Left-handed."

"Oh, my," she said. "But I was asking about the little boy. We have no Negro families around here."

"No idea. He sure was quick till he met up with Lefty Wheeler."

Lefty. That was it. Sarah gave another sigh. She stood up and said she would leave his washed and ironed handkerchief at the general store in Eastborough, if that would not inconvenience him. At least, the other side of her brain said, that would tell her whether he lived hereabouts or not. Silas opened his mouth to protest and then shut it again. He knew the store, knew the young fellow behind the counter, made deliveries there regular, and he'd find a way to find her again. Something told him it was important to find her again. Besides, how hard could it be? Eastborough was a pretty small town. But he wasn't even sure she actually lived there.

"Thank you," he said. "Pleasure to meet you." And before Sarah could say a word, he turned and walked off, disappearing between the booths. Sarah wondered if she would have to wrap the handkerchief or if she could just ask Henry Goodnow to take care of it. Henry was a nice young man, but he certainly would think it odd to be delivering laundry. She could do that because she considered him a friend, considerable older, but a friend. Besides, she was a little in awe of his father and the gruff way he greeted his customers. She pictured Henry handing over the "hanky" and laughed out loud. It was time to get on home, she thought, so she picked up her basket and made her way out of the fairgrounds, watching all the while for the people who had changed her afternoon – a small dark boy, someone named Silas Hibbard and a pitcher named Lefty. She saw none of them.

Sarah was so deep inside her head, where that little boy kept screaming, that she almost missed the dirt track leading to her house. She caught herself and turned in, choosing to walk on the left strip of dirt. She almost always walked on the dirt because the grass tickled if you were barefoot. And besides, she didn't want to step on any ants. Which sometimes bite. My feet, she thought, feel as if they were still at the fair. She stooped quickly and unlaced the boots her father had bought her for Christmas. They were a trifle tight, but she gave that no mind – they were grand and well-worn enough now to wear to the fairgrounds, where the paths tended to be muddy and slippery after the first day.

Who was that boy, she wondered, swinging her boots with one hand and her basket with the other. Silly, she told herself. Silas Hibbard, that is the who. But where? Where did he come from, and what kind of house did he grow up in? She'd never met a male person that age before who would think of stopping to comfort a stranger, lend a handkerchief, not turn red, nor stammer. This boy was different. She would launder the hanky and take it to Henry Goodnow, who was likely to know who Silas Hibbard was – well, who he was really. Meaning who was his mother. That would tell something.

She reached the kitchen door and went in. Her mother was in the rocker, snapping beans as fast as her fingers could move, quickly reducing the mountain in the trug. She let the stems and tails fall into her skirt and, without pausing, greeted Sarah and smiled at the sight of a full basket of fair goods.

"How was it, what did you purchase, was Priscilla there, were the quilts better than last year? Did Priscilla have an entry?" The words rattled out quicker than gunfire, and Sarah perched on the edge of the wood box to consider each and try to answer.

"The best ever, bits and pieces of fabric, yes, she was, no, the quilts were splendid but not prettier than last year, Priscilla had a log cabin with reds in solids and prints." She glanced down at her basket and was glad the handkerchief was out of sight. "They won't be putting the prize ribbons on until tomorrow," she added.

"Reckon we won't bring home one of them," her mother said matter-of-factly.

Sarah decided not to respond to that and asked, instead, "What shall I prepare for supper?"

"Biscuits, I reckon. We'll be having a mess of beans. Bread gets baked here so regular you'd think we'd never run out. But within hours, seems like, it's as scarce as hen's teeth. Drop them. Your father doesn't favor the cut ones."

Sarah nodded, wondering why anyone said "mess" about beans. They were so neat – long and slim and green with a stem on one end and a little tail on the other. She put away her boots and her basket, put on shoes and an apron and headed for the pantry where she could mix the flour, milk, shortening and leavening. She had about decided the oven would be hot enough to bake the biscuits without building up the fire when her mother's voice came from the kitchen. "No call for poking up the fire. The biscuits may take a few extra minutes, but mostly we need to cool down in here."

"Yes, Mother," Sarah called back. "Prob'ly won't rise quite as high, but that will do no harm."

A minute later she heard the back door open and shut again and knew Nell must be home from the fair, too. Her sister had to answer the same questions she had, and Sarah grinned as she realized her mother had fired them out in exactly the same order.

In a couple of minutes, Nell peered into the pantry and remarked in a teasing voice, "Quilt pieces? Ma says you bought bits of fabric? What I saw was you sitting on a rock with a young man. Tell, just tell. I won't tell, but you must."

"Oh, Nell, it was so awful I can't begin to talk about it yet."

Alarmed, her older sister came all the way into the pantry and pushed the door closed behind her. "He looked all right, so I didn't come to the rescue, Sarah. I'm so sorry, so sorry!"

"No, no, you have it all wrong. The awful part was before. The young man was the good part." She paused and added, "The sweet part."

"Sweet? Now you do need to tell."

"I'm finishing the biscuits first," Sarah said, reaching for the stained baking sheet and suddenly realizing that her sister was really interested in this tale. She'd make her wait. It wasn't often that Sarah had something to share that Nell really wanted. They'd sit on the porch, and she would tell the whole story. She blushed a little, thinking that the last part really was sweet.

Nell scowled, but she went back to the kitchen to get out dishes and flatware for supper. They'd need bowls for the beans and small plates for the biscuits. She knew Sarah made the best biscuits, but they were always so short that everyone made crumbs all over the tablecloth. She knew that Father would lick his finger and tap as many crumbs as he could reach and pop them into his mouth. She was disgusted by his lack of manners but admitted to herself that she never could take her eyes off the hunt. Thinking about it made her grin. It was amusing.

CHAPTER TWO

With his hands in his pockets, Silas Hibbard smiled as he strolled along the midway. He couldn't quite believe he'd walked up to a weeping girl and offered his hanky. And now, he hoped, he'd maneuvered a way to find out more about her. He stopped in front of the booth where the Negro boy had been smashed in the face and saw that a different, also colored, boy had taken his place and was successfully dodging baseballs, sometimes just by tipping his head down and letting the ball graze his head. That didn't count as a hit, Silas noticed. He s'posed the boy's thick hair provided a little protection. He also saw that, in spite of the gruesome scene only an hour or so earlier, young men were lining up to pay their quarter and get two baseballs. He moved on, thinking about Sarah again and suddenly realizing that he could leave her a note. Or his card. He had just had a few cards made so he could leave them with merchants who might give him a job. Goods, he'd learned young, had to be transported, and people paid. It was a lot more pleasant than working on his parents' farm all the time. And, truth be admitted, helped them keep that farm out of the hands of the lenders.

As he walked, another idea popped into his head. If she didn't respond to a note, he would show up at the next Eastborough square dance. At his town in Vermont, when you had your eye on a girl, it was plenty easy to get yourself placed as a corner in "Red River Valley" or across the way in a reel. Good lord, he told himself, you are scheming away just because a girl didn't like a cruel young man tricking a little kid. A pickaninny. No, a Negro, he corrected. His father sometimes used that other word, but his mother didn't like it. She said everyone should get respect, and it wasn't a respectful word. Huh, he thought. Good thing she wasn't at the fair today. Might have been more upset than Miss Sarah. He stopped at a booth and put down a quarter for five rings of different sizes. As if he were skipping stones at the lake, he sent them one after the other toward the row of glass bottles. Three hit, and the smiling man said he could pick whichever stuffed animal he wanted. He chose a brown bear with a red ribbon around his neck and decided to go home while he was winning. Mebbe he could give it to Sarah? You're a fool, he told himself. Probably never see her again. He'd give it to his little sister.

At the Sherman house, Sarah was already cutting the butter into the flour with two crossed table knives and still having trouble getting that injured dark-faced boy out of her mind. All the blood, the shrieks of pain and then, surprise, surprise, the appearance of the young man with a handkerchief. She'd wash it out tonight and iron it tomorrow. She reckoned she'd better find a private moment for the ironing. If her mother saw her heating up an iron for one handkerchief, she'd have questions. Sarah found herself not wanting to share information about meeting that nice young man – would he be considered man, or boy? –

this afternoon. She'd tell her mother about Lefty Wheeler instead. What a mean trickster he was and how that colored lad had howled when the baseball smacked him. She could still hear the sound in her head. She shook her head, willing the tears not to escape and pulled her mind back to the bowl in front of her. Had she added the salt? She wasn't sure. She sent her mind backward and remembered sprinkling a teaspoon or so into the mix. She had better stop thinking about the fair.

She dropped spoonsful of sticky batter on the cookie sheet and went back to the kitchen. When she opened the oven door, heat rushed at her, so she quickly popped the pan in, quite sure the biscuits would rise and bake without adding sticks to the fire.

"Set a spell," her mother said. "I want to hear all about the fair, and your father will only want to know about ox-pulling and the weight of the Gloucester pigs." So Sarah took the other rocking chair, grateful not to be alone with Nell just yet and started with the barn of quilts and other items made by their friends and neighbors.

"The antimacassars were quite unbelievable," she began, "especially ones made by a woman from Ripton. Hers were heart-shaped, very lacy and done in ecru cotton with a red border all around."

"Red? Even if it is a heart, red seems harsh."

"It was an off-red," Sarah said. "Soft."

She went on to describe cross-stitched scarves for bureaus and a knitting display that ranged from afghans to mittens. She had made a point to remember at least a few of the names because her mother knew just about everybody, even though she didn't get out much. She glanced now and then at the clock over the kitchen sink and in a few minutes stood up to check the biscuits. She took a toothpick from the little glass jar on the dining room table and poked it into one.

"Pretty high, but a little slow on the cooking," she said, holding out the toothpick with a sticky dough tip.

"Then you can go on," her mother said, her rocker creaking as she tipped her feet up and down. "Please."

So, Sarah finished describing the women's handwork displays and went on to the fruits and vegetables. The squashes a little small, overall, but everyone seemed to have beautiful summer apples and raspberries. "But none prettier than ours, I think," she added.

Her mother had finished snapping the beans and handed the pan to Sarah, who rinsed them off with water from the pail in the sink and then sighed.

"What is it?" Emma Sherman wanted to know.

"Going to have to poke up the fire for the beans anyway," Sarah said. "Hot or not."

"Just do it," her mother said. "We need to eat these nice and fresh, so cold supper is not possible tonight."

Sarah moved a lid aside on the wood stove and dropped two pieces of kindling into the fire. She replaced the lid, waited a bit and then opened the fire door to put in a couple of larger logs. The coals were glowing, so the kindling flared almost immediately. The beans would take a good half hour, and they would eat them in bowls with plenty of butter melting into the juice. She did love beans, so she would not fret about the fire. With the pot on to boil, she quickly removed the slightly browned biscuits. They smelled really fine.

She had just finished all this when Nell appeared at the kitchen door and beckoned. "Get along with you," her mother said. "I'm sure Nell wants to know who you saw and talked with at the fair. She gave me little information about what she did there."

So, Sarah went out to the porch, glad to escape the hot kitchen, and sat down to tell Nell about Silas Hibbard, the screaming colored boy and the handkerchief that must be laundered. She tried to be a good storyteller, so she was pleased to see Nell moving to the edge of her seat when she told how the pitcher had fooled the midway boy and how the child had bled and screamed while the high school boys laughed. She saw Nell start to open her mouth, but she closed it without speaking.

"I wanted to help, but I was useless, crying and making a spectacle of myself, so I ran behind the midway booths and sat down on a large boulder and bawled," Sarah said, her voice cracking as she saw the scene all over again.

"What a cruel boy," Nell said then. "Did you know him?"

"Thought he was familiar, but no. When Silas Hibbard came along, he knew. Said he was from Ripton and a star pitcher for the academy. A southpaw, he said."

"Who is Silas Hibbard? Where did you meet him? I ain't never heard that name. And what's a southpaw?"

"A left-handed pitcher," Sarah said and fell silent.

"Never mind about the pitcher, Sarah. Who is this Silas person?" Nell said, quite annoyed by her sister's dodging.

"Haven't ever seen him before," Sarah said, and wished she hadn't when she saw Nell's scowl. She went on quickly. "Met him at the rock. He saw me leave the midway crying, and he came after me and offered his handkerchief."

"So, you watched a crime and then you took a handkerchief from a stranger? Sarah, I reckon you are the oddest being."

"Well, he gave his name, so then he wasn't a stranger anymore, and he asked mine, and then he sat down on the rock to keep me company." Sarah hoped she wasn't going to blush, but just thinking about Silas Hibbard perching on the rock made her feel all warm inside.

"You, Sarah, are blushing. You are becoming a beet!"

Sarah tried to ignore her and added, "So I brought his hanky home …"

"You whaaaat?"

"I brought his handkerchief home because I promised to launder and iron it."

"And where does this boy on a white horse live? How will you return it?"

"He was not on a horse."

"Saaraah!"

"I'm to leave it at the store with Henry, and he'll pick it up. No need for me to meet him or anything."

"Except you'd like that, wouldn't you?" Nell was laughing now, forgetting the injured boy for the moment with this new interest and pleased she was finally getting the whole story from her sister.

"It was just a small favor, and I'm doing a favor in return," Sarah said rather primly. She stood and went to the kitchen to check on the beans, hoping Nell wouldn't bring up her story at the supper table. Nell leaned back in her chair and thought she could certainly find out where this remarkable boy lived. Not in their town, she already knew, but she'd find him. She sat up suddenly and said aloud, "Except he might find Sarah himself. If he was taken by her at all." She closed her eyes, hoping for even the tiniest breath of moving air. She smiled. Sarah had seen something perfectly awful, and now she was obviously smitten by the young man with a hanky. It was too delicious for words. But she'd just enjoy it herself. No need to repeat the tale over supper.

The sound of the cicadas in the locust trees and the sticky air made her suddenly drowsy, but she roused quickly when she heard her father's heavy step outside the kitchen door. She'd have to get up. He would have washed up outside and would be hungry as a fisher cat. She pulled herself up and headed for the kitchen where she found her father rather excitedly telling her mother about the accident at the fair.

"Didn't know you'd be getting there," Emma Sherman said.

"Didn't," Father replied. "Had to pick up a sharpener at the store and ran into Delbert Chandler. He'd just come from the midway, toting a large doll in a pink dress. He'd won it at the shooting gallery and was a sight to see toting it. He was full to the brim with the story about the little pickaninny getting bashed in the head by some fool kid from Ripton."

"Lefty Wheeler," Sarah said.

Her father turned quickly and wanted to know if she knew the fellow.

"No, sir," Sarah said. "But I was there, and others knew who he was." She paused, wondering if she should go on. "It was awful," she added, and she turned back to the stove where the mess of beans was bubbling away, her stomach suddenly going all funny.

Behind her, she heard her mother say, "I reckon it isn't proper to call a little Negro boy a pickaninny."

"Reckon you're right, Emma. My apologies. No one seemed to know where he came from so Delbert figured he was on the road. Apparently bled pretty good."

"And the boys from Ripton all laughed and walked away, Father," Sarah said without looking around. She was hoping to high heaven that Nell wouldn't add to this story. Just let everyone think about the baseball pitcher and the boy. She shuddered, hearing the shrieking again.

"I reckon that's a tad more than just 'boys will be boys,'" John Sherman said. "More like cruel. And he didn't stay to inquire about the picka-Negro." He frowned and added, "Not the Christian thing to do."

"Let's eat," Nell said, taking the large bowl of beans from Sarah to the dining room and giving her a small smile. Each place had a soup bowl, and Sarah brought in the steaming biscuits and a covered glass butter dish. She had already dropped a large chunk of butter into the beans, adding a yellow tint to the water in the bowl.

"Nothing like fresh beans for supper on a hot night," John said as he sat down and helped himself before handing the bowl across the table to his wife. "They going to produce steady for a while?" As Emma nodded, he put a large forkful in his mouth and reached for the tumbler of water at his place. It was ice cold, Sarah knew, because that was how he liked it, and her mother always put a container of water right against the block of ice in the icebox. No one else was allowed to drink that water, just Father. It was one of those things, she thought. Water from the well was pretty cool, even in summer, but he wanted cold. Said it washed barn dust out of his throat.

No one spoke for a time while they busied themselves with beans, biscuits and butter. Sarah knew her father would comment in a minute or two. The game she played with herself was whether he would say, "Nice and light," as crumbs fell from his moustache, or "I do like the drop ones best."

Right on time, he looked up from his bowl and said, "I do like the drop ones best," adding to her surprise, "Who put together this batch?"

"I did, sir," Sarah said.

"Right good."

High praise, Sarah knew. Was he being especially nice because of what she'd seen at the fair? She didn't know. What she did know was that she was expected to deal with the problem herself, not go caterwauling about with her grief for the little boy. No one in this family had a bent toward pats on the back. For praise or for comfort. She had learned to deal with that, although she often wished her family was more like Mary's. When Mary brought home her marks from school, she was asked to read the best ones aloud. Here, no one asked her to read hers. At the Sherman house, when Sarah's report showed success in everything, her mother would say something like, "I expect that from you," and her father would just say, "Ayuh," which meant he'd read it. Sometimes she wondered what they'd do if the teacher wrote, "Sarah is very difficult in the classroom."

"Sarah?" It was her mother's voice. "You've gone off somewhere. Your father wants to know if you looked over the vegetable exhibits or the sheep."

"Sorry, sir," Sarah said. "I just keep thinking about that poor little boy. Everyone's vegetables looked quite beautiful, but none better than ours. No ribbons have been awarded for those yet. I did go to the sheep barn, and the Barnes and Chandler families took most of the prizes there. In another barn, I saw a knot of people at one pen and found them all admiring our sow Matilda and her piglets."

"Did you tell 'em who you were?" her father asked.

"No, sir. They were all talking to each other. Do you think she'll get a ribbon? They didn't judge the pigs today."

"She's a prize pig, win or lose," John Sherman said, reaching for seconds on the beans. Sarah hoped for a blue ribbon. It had been a lot of trouble to get that big sow and her wriggling piglets into the wagon and safely delivered to the fair barns. As soon as everyone was finished, Nell and Sarah cleared the bowls and set an apple pie and a stack of plates in front of their mother. Once the pie was served, everyone fell silent again until the last crumb was gone. Then the sisters cleared again. As usual, they watched Father tilt his chair back a little and close his eyes. A full stomach,

Sarah thought, puts him right to sleep for a short spell, but how is it that he never goes over backwards? Carefully, so's not to wake him, she scraped up a few stray crumbs with a table knife. She was trying to think how she could get the handkerchief washed without anyone noticing when Nell poked her in the ribs.

"Ouch," Sarah said.

"Ssssh," Nell hissed. "I saved back hot water from the dishes so you could get that hanky clean. Do it now while no one is paying attention." Sarah quickly dipped the handkerchief in the hot water, swished it around and figured it no longer had any salty tears in it. Certain sure it couldn't be considered dirty. She wrung it out at the sink while Nell shielded her from view, and then went upstairs to her room to find a place where it could dry. Hanging it out of sight under a towel on the washstand, she started to giggle. All this fuss over a young man's hanky. But would she ever see him again? She hoped so. But how? She'd been pondering that ever since he'd disappeared into the midway.

Back downstairs, she grinned her thanks at Nell and whispered, "How do I manage the ironing part?"

"Stay up late," Nell advised. "Are you going to write a note when you leave it at the store?"

Sarah had thought of that. She wanted to write something, something that would bring another meeting with this new boy. But her mind was a blank at the moment. She wondered if he'd think her very forward if she wrote. Nice girls weren't forward, she knew. Her mother and the minister had both made that clear. She was supposed to be more of a mouse than a cat.

"No pouncing," she said out loud without thinking.

"What's that?" Nell asked.

Sarah felt herself blushing but quickly answered, "I'm not supposed to act like a cat. We are all just mice."

"And hoping to be caught one day," Nell laughed. "You are a strange one sometimes."

"Mebbe. But I think in another life I'd like to be a cat."

Nell looked at her in wonder. "Very strange. But Mother will be out to the garden early tomorrow, so you'll have a chance to heat an iron and get that piece of linen fixed up fine. You could tear a piece of paper out of your composition book to wrap it and tie it with a string. I can't begin to think what our friend Henry will think of these goings-on."

"He won't tell anyone. We know that," Sarah said, and the two girls giggled. Henry sometimes sneaked them two pieces of penny candy without asking for the pennies. In return, they helped him with his reading now and then. He could count out change quick as a wink, but he stumbled over a passel of words in school, even though he was one of the oldest boys there. Turned out his father had taught him all the coins as soon as he turned three, but no one read him any books. Sarah and Nell were the opposite. Their mother and father had few coins to their name, but they had a whole shelf of books, and every Sunday afternoon the family sat down for reading aloud. Emma Sherman had strict rules about Sundays. No chores except feeding and watering and mucking out. No cards. No piano or singing except hymns. The reading was thus welcome all around, exactly as she intended but never admitted.

By the time they went to school, both girls could read from "The Last of the Mohicans," and when they made up their little plays out under the apple trees in summer, they argued every time about who would be the brave Hawkeye and who one of the timid women he was supposed to guard against fierce Indians in war paint and mysterious soldiers from faraway France.

The next morning, as soon as her mother took down a basket and headed for the garden, Sarah set a flat iron on the hot stove and spread a piece of an old flannel blanket and two pillow slips on the dining room table. She fetched the handkerchief, which was thankfully still a little damp, and her square-dancing skirt, which she reckoned would be an excuse for ironing. The next church supper and dance were two weeks away, but she knew Mother would think nothing amiss if she came back too soon.

Humming to herself, Sarah ironed the handkerchief and suddenly heard her mother's footsteps on the stairs. She quickly spread her skirt over her secret and went on circling the skirt. She didn't turn around, knowing her face would have that guilty look her mother always recognized instantly.

"Too wet," her mother said, "to pick beans. Heavy dew last night with fairy sheets all over the grass. Your father won't like the damp on the hay he mowed two days ago, but it's grand for the garden."

"You believe in fairies?" Sarah asked in surprise.

"Not really," Emma said with a chuckle. "But it's a nice story and much more pleasant than imagining some bug spitting out those webs. Aren't you a little ahead of yourself there with the square dance still two weeks off?"

Sarah nodded. "But the stove was hot and the day still cool, Mother. It seemed like a good time."

"At least one of you seems to be a planner," Emma said. "Perhaps you've time to do a shirtwaist for me?"

"Certainly," Sarah nodded. She ran the iron firmly over the place where the handkerchief was hidden. Hidden in plain sight, she thought. Now she understood that saying. As soon as her mother went upstairs to get her clothes for ironing she pulled out the hanky, ran over it again – she wouldn't leave a single wrinkle – and quickly folded it into a small square that fit in her apron pocket. Skirt over her arm, she ran upstairs to hang it up and wrap the handkerchief in a sheet of paper from her composition book. Nell did think of everything. On the inside of the wrapping, she quickly wrote, "I thank you again. S." She tied a string around the package and tucked it in her skirt pocket. If only Mother would send her to the store today.

Luck was with her. As soon as she reappeared in the kitchen, her mother said, "Long's it's wet out and still not hot, you could get yourself to Mr. Goodnow's once you take care of my shirtwaist. Pick up a few things and put them on the charge there. We've little enough cash in the sugar bowl."

Sarah found a scrap of paper and a stub of pencil, made a list, ironed her mother's things and set out, walking quickly and feeling light as air. Silas's handsome face was in her mind's eye, and she was so concentrated on the picture that she tripped over a large rock and felt a half second of sharp pain in her big toe. She'd have to take to wearing shoes all the time if she couldn't keep her mind on what she was doing, she thought. But her mental eye went right back to that smiling face, and she felt an odd shiver run down her spine. In almost no time, she was at the store. What if young Henry wasn't there? What if she stammered and blushed? It's just a hanky, she told herself sternly, and you are returning it to the owner.

She climbed the steps and went inside the store, into the magic place where the smell of straw, flour, chicken feed, fresh-cut stove wood and newly baked brown bread mixed together more or less harmoniously. She did love the store, especially the part that had no aroma at all – the button cabinet. She never could believe how many buttons lived there, black and white and brown and even a few blue and red ones. And one or two samples of buttons with jewel stones in them. She never asked, but she had an idea they weren't real stones. Mr. Goodnow wouldn't leave them out like that if they were diamonds or sapphires.

"Good morning, Sarah," a quiet voice said behind her. "You are out with the robins today."

"Hello, Henry," she answered. "But I don't want any worms."

"We have 'em," the boy said cheerfully. "Keep 'em in the icebox so they'll be lively when the fishermen put 'em on the hook."

"Separate from the milk, I trust," Sarah said, laughing and no longer anxious. "I have this little packet, Henry, and I'm in hopes you'll keep it in a secret place until a young man comes to fetch it."

"Whatever you need, Sarah," he answered quickly. "But

this sounds like a story you haven't told yet. And how will I know if he's the right one if you tell me nothing?"

"And not going to," she said saucily. "His name is Silas, and he'll be calling for it."

Henry sighed and reached out his hand. Sarah took the packet from her skirt pocket and gave it to him. He hefted it, sniffed it and shook his head. "Can't imagine," he said. "But I'll take care of it."

"Without opening it."

"Yes, ma'am. Cross my heart."

Sarah turned to go and heard Henry clear his throat and ask, "You and Nell going to the square dance?"

She knew he really only wanted to know about Nell, but she said, "I've already ironed my skirt, sir," and continued toward the door. Then she remembered he was doing her a favor, so she said over her shoulder, "And Nell always goes. She's just behind on the ironing."

CHAPTER THREE

Silas Hibbard hopped down from the wagon seat and tied his horse to a post in front of the train station. The sun was barely up, but he would need all the daylight he could get to finish the job he faced this day. Mr. Goodnow, way over the mountain in Eastborough, wanted to put some sizable glass panes on his storefront, and Silas was getting the newly made sheets off the train from New Hampshire. Seems the conductor on the train that connected to Eastborough wouldn't take a chance on carrying that glass, not even for an extra bit of cash. And had added that it was a danged fool idea anyway.

Silas knew that store in Eastborough. He'd known it even before he'd loaned his handkerchief to a crying girl. The whole storefront was pretty much closed in, a two-story wall of rather faded clapboards. He understood a carpenter was cutting three large holes in the face of the building because Mr. Goodnow had read a newspaper account of how some fancy city stores were arranging their wares behind glass so people on the street would stop, look and be tempted to come in and buy. Silas had told his mother the story when he agreed to transport the glass, and she had chuckled and muttered something about a fool being born every time the sun came up. But Silas did know that store and its dark interior, where the odor of smoke from the pot-bellied stove hung over everything like an invisible curtain. Still, it was so clean, the shelves dusted and the sawdust on the floor quite fresh. You could get whatever you might want and some things you didn't even need. He could see where the windows would make it bright inside, and he had a feeling that would move the merchandise. He shook his head, telling himself that he had no idea about anything in the store business, but he was grateful for this job because perhaps, just perhaps, he'd find his handkerchief there.

He carried the glass to his wagon and set the sheets against one wheel. He pushed aside some of the straw he had packed that morning and laid in one sheet of glass, covering it with straw. Then another the same way. Once all three panes – he had never seen glass pieces that large before – were in place, he pulled a thick blanket from under the seat and spread it over the top. He'd be going over the mountain on a road rutted by rain, and this was a cargo not to be jostled. If the panes broke, his day was wasted. The man who hired him said he'd pay when he saw a note from Mr. Goodnow that all was well.

It was a chance he had to take because three weeks had gone by since the county fair. Three weeks when that girl's face had kept pushing its way into his thoughts. He reckoned Miss Place, the teacher who set such store by vocabulary lists, would say he was pining. Getting this cargo over the mountain road meant risking sudden ownership of a pile of shattered glass, but he realized he was looking forward to the challenge. He'd seen more than a little doubt on the faces of the men who saw him loading the glass. He grinned. He'd do it. And hope to get his hanky back. She won't be there, but if the hanky was, perhaps there'd be a note. He wasn't much on writing, but he'd borrowed a sheet of paper from his mother and scrawled thank you and signed his name. He'd also have a word with the storekeeper about what shindigs might be in the offing in the village. Surely, she'd be at any social event, pretty girl like that. He wished he'd worked a little harder at penmanship, all those A's and B's on line after line, but it was water over the dam. And the stationery had a couple of flowers on it. He should have said it was borrowed.

Satisfied that the glass was quite safe, Silas untied Dolly and hopped onto the wagon seat. He whistled two notes, and the horse began to move. He had guided her slightly left so the wheels would roll on the shoulder and the center of the road. He reckoned the horse could manage the rutted track, and the wheels would roll easy. The morning quiet was suddenly pierced by the whistle of the train that had delivered the glass. And then, in a minute or two, they had left the town behind and were alone on the bumpy gravel road that would soon start to rise steeply and go over North Mountain. He was confident about the ascent, knowing he had to keep the horse moving so the wagon had no way to roll back, but he was not quite sure how to handle the descent. All he knew was he couldn't give Dolly her head. He needed her to dig in and take it slow. He let out a long breath and decided not to think about that part yet. He had to do it.

An hour later, he reached the summit and guided Dolly toward a healthy clump of grass on the roadside. He dropped the reins, a signal she knew meant she should stop. Quickly, she lowered her head and put her long teeth into the patch of grass. Silas jumped down and checked his cargo. All appeared to be well. The plate glass had not shifted so much as an inch. He reached behind the seat for the milk can he had filled with water, unhooked the bucket he always carried and filled it. The water wasn't cool like it was from the spring, but Dolly immediately plunged her velvety nose in and drank noisily. Looking around him, Silas let out a long breath. Half a problem solved.

He knew perfectly well that his habit of conversing with animals made him a figure of fun in his family. Or even in town, if he hitched Dolly to a post and had a little talk with her before going on his errands. But he went to her head now, held her bridle and explained the next part of the trip to her. She tossed her head to get free of his hand, bent to get another mouthful of grass and then gave a small whinny. Message delivered, he thought, and chuckled. Good thing he was alone.

He moved slowly toward the wagon seat, hoping to convince Dolly that this wasn't a horse race. And so they started down North Mountain, a considerable number of miles to go. The horse seemed to be leaning back a bit, pushing her front legs out and her haunches back. Carry that all the way, girl, and you'll be sitting down, he thought. But he knew it was working, and the horse was certainly working at it. Her flanks were wet with sweat now, and once in a while she gave a snort. The wagon rolled steadily but very slowly down the mountain, small stones popping as the wheels turned and the horse's shoes clicking on the occasional larger rock. He'd earn enough on this trip to make the next monthly payment to the man who all but owned their farm. He frowned, thinking with a touch of anger about his father slipping into debt. He hated the long tab he saw when he bought flour and salt for his mother, and he couldn't help feeling, sometimes, that his father had failed them. Didn't work hard enough? Didn't see the opportunities? He didn't know. But he had no intention of following in his footsteps. He was going to own a farm of his own and do well enough so he really owned it. He would not live on the edge of a cliff as his parents did. Not that many others weren't in the same fix.

Then the steeple of the Eastborough Church cut into the view, and he let out a long breath. They had made it. His gloomy thoughts fell away, disappearing as if the clang of the church bell had drowned them out. He wondered idly why a bell would ring now. He had lost track of time, obsessed with the notion that a note would come with a clean, ironed hanky. He passed the hotel and the train station and hoped it wasn't so late in the day that Mr. Goodnow would have closed his doors. Ah, that was why the bell rang – it was the end of the day. He wondered if everyone here was very pious, something he'd never quite understood. He tugged on the left rein, and Dolly turned into the road next to the Goodnow store. When he whistled, she came to a stop, and he jumped down and hurried to the wagon bed to see if the glass was intact. He was brushing a layer of straw aside when young Henry appeared.

"The glass?" he said. "You have it?"

"All of a piece, far as I can see," Silas said, grinning at him.

"I must tell Father," the boy said, running back into the store. He took the steps two at a time and then turned on the porch to say in a sly voice, "Got something for you here, too."

Silas felt an odd crunch in his chest. Sarah, he thought. Mebbe. He'd better tend to business here and not be getting the flutters like some girl at her first dance. He leaned against the wagon and waited for Mr. Goodnow to come out and inspect the merchandise. Then he'd head for home, grateful that his family's farm was on this side of the mountain. It'd be dark before he could get there, but it wasn't a tough road. Rough but not tough, he reckoned.

The Goodnows, son and father, came out and carefully pulled the straw layers away, lifted the glass and carried the sheets into the store. When Mr. Goodnow came back, he stretched a hand to Silas.

"Proud to make your acquaintance, young man. That was a remarkable feat," he said. "Warn't certain it could be done, but you packed 'em like eggs. My wife's been looking forward to those windows and the chance to arrange everything from buttons to fertilizer where those walking past can see what we do here. 'Spect they'll create quite a flurry."

"Pleased to do it, sir," Silas said. "The horse did her job, too, holding back all the way down North Mountain." Mr. Goodnow looked at Silas appraisingly. "Like to have seen that," he said. Then the two shook hands again, and Silas allowed as how he would like to get a bite at the hotel and could he get water for the horse and let her just stand for a few minutes.

"Whatever you need," Mr. Goodnow said. "I'll have young Henry bring out a bucket. As soon as he went back inside, young Henry appeared with a packet in his hand. "For you, she told me. Cross my heart and not open it, nor breathe a word." Eyes on the ground, he held out the package.

Silas nodded, took it and thanked him, who was in reality about his age he reckoned. He wondered how long you had to be referred to as "young Henry" – did your father have to die? He decided he'd never name a child of his for himself. He crossed over to the hotel and asked for a mug of tea and whatever breadstuffs they had with a little butter. He looked down at what was in his hand and felt that weird twist in his chest again. The hotel was pretty much deserted at this time of day, but he held the packet in his lap while he unfolded it. A clean handkerchief. And nicely ironed. He'd be saving this one for Sunday go to meeting time. He unfolded the paper all the way and there it was, the short note. Really short, he thought, but he meant to attach no meanin' to its length. His tea came and he wrapped his hands around the hot mug. Then he slurped up a spoonful and spread a little butter on the thick slice of oatmeal bread. While he ate, he chewed on what to do next. First, he needed a slip from Mr. Goodnow saying the glass had arrived in one piece. Three pieces, actually. He wondered if he could ask in the store about square dances. Well, why not. He'd get on back and collect his pay.

Silas put two ten-cent pieces on the table and pushed back his chair. Back at the store, he pawed through the drawer of white buttons and picked out two that he thought his mother could use on shirts. Nearly every night she sat near the stove with the mending, turning a frayed collar, painstakingly fixing a hole in a sock or searching through her button box for one that matched the others on a shirt. He went to pay, and Mr. Goodnow asked if he wanted to run a tab. He said not at present and put the buttons on the counter. After he paid for them, he asked, "Does Eastborough have a square dance now and then? My town rarely has such, and I would come back this way for that."

"Coming up in a fortnight," Mr. Goodnow said. "Right over at the Town Hall."

"Stable for my horse?" Silas asked.

"Right behind the store, and if you don't mind roughing it, you could sleep in the mow. Reckon you'd want to stay over till morning?"

"No, sir. Dolly doesn't mind a night run, and I need to be back for chores." He paused and added, "Anything you need delivered over my way?"

"Not today, young man, but I'll keep you in mind. That was a risky job you took today, and you did well. I have written out a note here affirming the goods delivered."

"Appreciate it, sir. Am I out of line to ask if I should see you in a fortnight about any future business?"

"Heck, no. And you'd be smart to come dancing. We have some capable young ladies here if you're not already committed. Some good-looking ones," he said with a chuckle.

Silas raised his hand in a wave, nodded and left the store. He and Dolly had a long way home, but he knew, if he showed her the way, his horse would make her way even in the dark. She gave a small snort as he approached to untie her reins, backed up quickly when he was seated and headed back the way they had come. He fingered the note and handkerchief in his pocket and once again felt that odd tingle in his spine. Or was it his stomach? He hadn't had much to eat this day. He sure hoped Sarah Sherman was a square dancer. It had been a long and satisfactory day. He allowed his body to unwind a little, and soon he dozed off, lulled by the rhythm of the wagon wheels, despite the many depressions in the road.

CHAPTER FOUR

"Primping?" Nell teased as she found her sister brushing her hair over and over in front of the glass. She watched in satisfaction as the pink color washed over Sarah's face and deepened. "Do you think your young man might be there tonight?"

"Not my young man, you goose," Sarah answered, continuing to brush her hair, which was already smooth and shiny.

"But you have to allow an interest," Nell answered, sure she'd struck a chord.

"He was so nice," Sarah sighed. "I hope he hasn't disappeared from my life."

"Not vanished," Nell said confidently. "You're not bad yourself, you know. If he's not a fool, he'll show up somewhere."

"He did leave a small note with Henry," Sarah confessed.

"And you kept *that* to yourself," Nell accused.

"And," Sarah added, her head down now, "he asked Mr. Goodnow about Eastborough events."

"Events, indeed. I am chaperoning you tonight."

"Nell," Sarah wailed. "Leave me alone."

"Ay-yuh," Nell said. "Going to put on my finery now."

Sarah sighed, fluffed out her square dance skirt and its petticoat, and decided to wear her favorite pin, a small pink gold one with pearls, at the collar of her shirtwaist. She buttoned her shoes and ran down the stairs to see if it was time to go. Suddenly, thinking about actually going, she felt a little breathless. What was the matter with her? All she'd done was bawl and attract attention and iron a handkerchief. Well, she thought with a small grin, it was an interesting combination of things.

Father had pulled up the wagon in the side yard and put down a box to make it easier for them to get in. He had put in the bench so the girls would have a real seat, and he had made room for Emma up front with him. Sarah noticed that he held out his hand to her mother, even though she was perfectly capable of getting herself into the wagon. That was nice, she thought. Gentlemanly. She made a mental note to bring that picture to mind again when he belched at table or had mashed potatoes stuck in his mustache.

When they arrived at Town Hall, John Sherman pulled up in front to let the ladies off, then drove around back where wagons and horses were clustered, some of the horses tethered to trees and others standing quietly, still hitched to their wagons. He jumped down, threw the reins over Billy's neck and brushed a little dust off his trousers. He could hear the caller starting a Virginia reel, so he hurried into the hall. Emma was partial to reels, and he was at her side just in time. Quickly they took their place at the end of one of the lines.

Nell and Sarah partnered in a group near their parents, not waiting for any of the young men to start dancing. At every dance, the boys and single men tended to gather near the table with food and pretended they had no interest in dancing. The sisters' private game was to pick the dance when the boys would get up the courage to join in.

"I am betting on the third dance," Nell said.

"Betting is a sin," Sarah answered. "I'll take the second because it's a line dance, and you don't have to put your arm around anyone." They both laughed as they glided through the reel couples and took their places at the end again, bowing and moving forward and back. And then Sarah, looking past Nell's shoulders, saw Silas joining the young men at the front of the hall. A wave of excitement swept over her, and Nell, seeing the odd look on her face, paused in mid-step and turned her head. She grabbed Sarah's arm.

"He's here. You just saw him. I saw you see him," she said. "Which one?"

"You saw me see him? You are such a goose, Nell."

"Goose or not, you are getting very pink."

Sarah looked down, concentrating on her feet and hoping only Nell had seen her face. Then all the hands were up in an arch, and it was the sisters' turn to dance through to the opposite end. "We'll land right near them," Sarah muttered, so softly she was certain she could not be heard above the music.

But Nell heard her and gave a triumphant little laugh. "Heard you," she teased, "and he saw you!" And then the music stopped, the fiddler put down his bow, and the groups broke up, most people lining up at the refreshment table for lemonade or a glass of Mrs. Chandler's rhubarb punch. When Sarah looked up, Silas was no longer there. She wanted to whirl around and search the room, but instead she gave in to Nell, who was pulling her toward the food tables.

"Rhubarb punch," Nell said. "My favorite." They took their places at the end of a short line and were almost to Mrs. Chandler when a voice behind them said, "Should I get lemonade or the pink one?"

"The pink one," Nell said quickly over her shoulder, realizing Sarah seemed to be frozen in place. "It's rhubarb. Famous in these parts, so you must be from some other parts."

Silas laughed, and Sarah turned, smiled at him and said, "This impertinent person is my sister. Nell, meet Silas Hibbard, Silas, meet Nell Sherman."

"Pleasure, I'm sure. And indeed, I am from somewhere else."

That made Nell laugh. She picked up a cup and held it out while Mrs. Chandler poured a dipperful for her, a second for Sarah, the third for Silas. Then Nell put three filled cookies on a plate and led the way to a small table, hoping the other two would follow. She reckoned she could leave them in a few minutes with some excuse, but she reckoned Sarah might indeed need a little company at the moment. Suppose she couldn't get a word out? All three were silent for a minute, then they all started to talk at the same time. That made each laugh a little too heartily, and Silas said, "I went to another fair, Miss Sarah, and the same midway was there, with the same baseball game."

"Oh, was the little Negro boy there?" Sarah cried, forgetting all about being shy.

"Indeed. With stitches on his head and a bandage. And still sticking his head out of that hole."

"That's just dreadful," Sarah said.

"He needs three squares a day like everyone else," Silas said. "Boss man seemed to think the bandage was bringing on more trade!"

"Disgusting," Nell said. "Really disgusting. Making money on that wound." She saw the surprise on Silas's face and added, "Sarah told us about that boy. It was the talk of the town, actually, for several days, so she had to tell the story over and over. Lefty Wheeler won't get much of a welcome around here for a while."

"Known to have a mean streak," Silas said. He took a long swallow of his drink and added, "Rhubarb packs a punch."

"You are funny," Nell said with a giggle, noticing that Sarah had apparently totally lost the power of speech.

"And a fine dancer," he said. "Will you join me on the next square, Miss Sarah?"

She looked up then and nodded, glancing toward the small platform where the fiddler stood. He was standing, picking at the strings on his fiddle and making small turns of the various knobs. "He's tuning," she said. "Perhaps he'll call a square soon." She smiled at Silas, but her head was swirling with thoughts that kept bumping into each other. He was really nice looking, would her dancing be good enough, her stomach felt funny from the punch, would Nell let them be alone. And why was she thinking about that?

Then she felt his calloused hand take hers. "He's ready," Silas said, smiling down at her. "Are you?"

"Ready," Sarah said, hoping her voice wasn't coming out in a squeak.

"Me, too," Nell said. "Save me a corner while I round up a partner."

Minutes later she found their square, and to Sarah's surprise, she was accompanied by one of their cousins, a gangly young man who was a couple of years older than Nell. "Meet John," Nell said, looking at Silas. "This is Silas from somewhere else," she told John, giggling and moving into the spot opposite Sarah and Silas. Then the fiddle began, the caller singing out the instructions, and the dancers starting to move. Soon arms were linked, wide skirts were whirling, feet were tapping, and everyone on the sidelines was clapping in time, the men stealing glances at the ladies' legs, usually hidden by layers of fabric. This is just plain happy time, Sarah thought, as she skipped through a grand right and left and rejoined Silas for a swing that took her right off her feet.

She was breathless but laughing when the fiddle stopped and everyone stood still. But the caller was wound up as tight as the chime clock on Sunday evening, and he started right in again with a new dance. One of the squares melted away, its older dancers ready for punch and a rest. But one of the younger men whooped, which brought echoes from around the room, and they were off again, gracefully executing a do-si-do with their corners, then exchanging bows with their opposites. Sarah was grateful that she had to listen, couldn't talk. She had no idea, now that she wasn't crying on a rock, what she might say to this young man. She had to admit, as he lightly guided her forward and back, that she liked his touch on her back.

When the music stopped, the caller took a deep breath, put his fiddle aside and asked the men to step to his left, the women to his right. "We're going to try a grand promenade," he said in his deep baritone voice, "and find out what you folks are made of."

Everyone clapped, the young man who had whooped before let out another yelp, and the men and women quickly separated. "It's not Puritan church, folks," the fiddler said. "I want the last man in the back to take the arm of the nearest lady and march forward, followed by one pair after another. At the front, the first pair turns right, the second to the left. When those four meet, they promenade toward me. Et cetera, et cetera, et cetera. We begin!" He jammed his fiddle under his chin and started to play.

Few were smiling as they went over the instructions in their minds. But the music was catchy, and suddenly Nell was there, taking the arm of the nearest man and, giving him a smile, starting to walk toward the fiddler, who had swung into a rollicking version of "Camptown Races."

He nodded to Nell and hollered, "In time, in time." She laughed, glanced at her partner and started to sway from side to side and stamp her feet on the "Doo-dah" parts of the familiar tune. He laughed and copied her odd gait as they neared the stage. Behind them came other pairs, also starting to smile and dance their way forward. Then they were in fours and, soon, in eights. Sarah had lost sight of Silas but thought this was the most entertaining caller they'd ever had. She linked arms with the nearest man and set off, immediately imitating her sister. In no time, they were a dozen pairs across and forming a second tier, then a third. And as quickly as it started, the music stopped, the lines nearly wall-to-wall.

"Sing it out, people! Sing it out!" the caller shouted. And he rolled into the song again while the crowd sang, the room filling with the shouts of "Doo-dah, doo-dah day!" Then the fiddle stopped, the caller said they were a remarkable group, and everyone headed for the punch table, talking and laughing together. Sarah's temporary partner bowed to her slightly and left her, but Nell had latched onto her new companion and was exchanging names with him. She saw Sarah and introduced her to the young man named Jason, who turned out to be the one who had whooped.

"Let's get a breath of air," Nell said, pushing Sarah toward the door. Despite her desire to find Silas again, Sarah went outside, followed by Nell and Jason. The night was cool, quite a change from the room where dancing people had created too much heat. Sarah tried to listen as Nell and Jason began to talk about things like the weather and who won prizes at the fair and whether they'd bring in as much feed corn as usual this year. But her eyes were everywhere, looking for Silas. If she had been impolite enough to turn around, she would have seen him looking for her, but instead she was startled when he came up behind her and touched her shoulder so lightly that his hand might have been a feather. Even so, it sent an unfamiliar wave of feeling through her. She knew the pink color was rising in her cheeks, but thank the lord it was too dark for anyone to see. Nell, however, gave her a knowing look as Sarah turned to greet Silas again.

Then she felt his breath on her neck as he leaned down and whispered in her ear, "I wish to ask your father if I may call on you. Do you mind?"

"Mind?" Sarah said aloud, turning toward him, hoping her voice wouldn't shake. "Why would I mind?"

"Reckon I can't answer that," he said. "I do want to be handy now and then if you need a clean handkerchief."

Sarah felt her body relax into a laugh. "Not usually a crier," she said softly. "Shall I point out my father?" She glanced around the room, not finding her father but conscious that Nell had heard the exchange and was grinning like Lewis Carroll's cat. Oh, she did hope Silas hadn't taken note of Nell. Then she saw her father's slightly stooped tall frame coming through the far door. "There," she said, "he's just coming in the door. Full head of hair and white shirt."

"Full head of hair?" Silas said, laughing.

Sarah blushed. "He makes fun sometimes of men who have what he calls 'shiny heads,'" she answered. "It's not nice, I know, but we always know he's going to say it."

"So, I can proceed?" Silas said rather stiffly. And then, running his hand over his head, adding, "Since I have many hairs on my head?"

Sarah looked at the floor, then glanced toward the spot where Nell had been standing. She was no longer there, nor was the young man named Jason. She smoothed her skirt and forced herself to look at Silas, who was shifting from one foot to the other. He's a little nervous, she thought.

"Yes," she said and felt her face flame again. Before she could say another word, he was gone, heading straight for the corner of the room where her father had rejoined several other men. His back was to her, so she could not read his lips, but her father looked up, his eyes circling the room until he found her. She nodded and saw him smile at Silas and say something. Then they shook hands, and Silas started back to her.

"Let's take a walk," he said abruptly as he reached her.

"Walk?" Sarah asked. "Where to?"

"Outside," he said, putting his hand under her elbow and turning her toward the back door. She shrugged his hand off, thinking they'd just been outside, hadn't they, but walked with him toward the door. It led, she knew, to a line of hitching posts and, a bit farther on, an open shed where horses could also be tied up. She felt a little apprehensive about being alone with this young man she hardly knew, but she'd seen her father smile. And she knew "call on you" meant "courting." She didn't know if she wanted to be courted.

Outside, Silas headed for a wooden bench set against the building. He made a grand gesture with his hand inviting her to sit, and she sat. Then he sat. Neither of them spoke for several minutes and then Silas said, "I really do want to see you regular, but I live a good way from here."

"You seem to have a handle on figuring things out," Sarah said. "You've already moved from a handkerchief for a bawling girl to introducing yourself to her father. In a matter of weeks." That made them both look at each other and laugh.

"I like you," Silas said. "I want to know more about you."

"Not much to know," Sarah answered. "I've lived here all my life – so far – and I do chores, listen to the preacher on Sunday with very little squirming and make my own clothes. Once in a great while, I get a chance to spend a day in town. Or," she said frowning, "go to a fair and see a boy get smashed in the head."

"My lucky day," Silas said, thinking she was prettier than ever tonight, not that he'd seen her that many times. "We'd better walk a little," he added, realizing that what he really wanted to do was kiss her, and he feared he'd scare her to death with that. He stood, reached for her hand to pull her up and then let go immediately. He felt her shiver when his fingers touched hers, but he didn't say anything. It certainly wasn't cold.

Feeling that fleeting tremble, Sarah wondered what was wrong with her. It wasn't cold. Could a boy's hand make you shiver? She didn't know, but she suggested they walk toward the road where they could see Mrs. Wellspeak's gardens. "Mostly white," she explained, "because she wants to see the flowers at night."

Silas didn't care where they went and kept looking sideways at Sarah as they strolled toward the house across the road. He was pleased as punch that he'd managed to be alone with her. If he had to look at flowers, he could do that. It had never crossed his mind that people planted flowers of a certain color so they could see them at night. Did this Wellspeak woman walk in the garden at night or just peer out the window? At least the sister and the father were no longer keeping an eye on them. He wondered if he could reach for her hand again and decided not to risk it. Just look at the flowers. White flowers.

Sarah wished he would take her hand again. She had liked that brief touch and the feeling it brought on. She kept her arms by her side and walked on, but he made no move toward her. She pointed out the dianthus in the garden and the tall, white phlox, both of which showed very white in the darkness. Then she said, thinking she might be boring him to death, "Do you like flowers?"

"Do," he answered. "But my mother doesn't have a flower garden. Prob'bly 'cuz she hasn't time with all the chores she has, chickens and all. And Minnie." And my father's neglect of so many things, he added to himself.

"Minnie?" Sarah said.

"My little sister. She's a piece of work. Forever running off."

"Running away?"

"Lord, no. Just hiding behind the chicken house and waiting for someone to find her. Quite amusing if you're not the one sent to look." Sarah said nothing, thinking about the older sister who was often a trial to her. Mebbe that's what it was like for everybody.

Now he did reach for her hand and turned her toward the dim light of the town hall where they were quickly pulled into a new square by Nell, who was still partnered with the handsome young man named Jason Harris. Sarah's corner was Mr. Goodnow, who turned out to be a superb dancer, and for a few minutes she managed to forget the shy feeling she had about Silas and just enjoy the music. Suddenly, the caller announced a final set, and the sisters kept their same places. Then it was over, and Silas shook hands with Jason and nodded to Nell. Then he did take Sarah's hand and headed toward the door. On the steps he paused and said, "I have permission to see you, so I will, if you agree."

Suddenly feeling very shy, Sarah looked down and then told herself to look up. "I agree," she said softly. "Will it be days, weeks, months?"

That made him laugh. "Days," he said and was gone.

CHAPTER FIVE

Silas broke into a trot toward the stable where he had left his horse and buggy. It was a long, dark road home, but he'd make it before milking time, maybe even in time for a little sleep. At least Dolly had gone this way before, and once they reached the fork in Fair Brook, she'd be eager to get home. He looked forward to getting a little sleep and not rousing until they were at the barn door.

He had it right. The moon had traveled a long way when the buggy stopped abruptly and Silas's head jerked up. The barn door was barely visible, but they were home. And the sun wasn't about to push the moon away quite yet. He hopped down, rolled the door to the side, unhitched Dolly and led her to her stall. He gave her feed and water and then went to check on the cows, wondering why a couple of them were blatting.

He looked down the long row of swishing tails and swore. Behind every cow was a pile of manure large enough to make him sure no shoveling had been done a'tall since he left. He slammed his fist against the wall, his happy mood gone, and bent down to check the udder on the nearest animal. Her bag was heavy. Not milked last night. They were blatting because they were hungry, he'd wager. Not milked, not fed.

"Judas priest, what in hell is going on here?"

The cows looked over their shoulders at the sound of his voice, and he fought the temper that was building fast in his head. Peace and quiet was what these ladies liked. Peace and quiet, his grandfather always said, was what made the milk sweet and the cream thick. He looked down at his square-dancing outfit and went back to Dolly's stall where he had a habit of keeping a spare cover-all. He pulled it on over his dress trousers, fetched a pail of grain and scattered small amounts in front of each cow. Noisily, they started to eat, not the least put off by the hour. Then he took a stool and a pail and perched by the nearest cow and started to milk.

He was still so angry that his hands were shaking, and the cow sidestepped away from him. Peace and quiet, he told himself, patting her flank and trying again. This time the milk came, and once her udder was slimmed down enough, he moved to the next animal, resting his forehead against her flank, the muscles in his forearms swelling and subsiding as his fingers pulled the milk.

"Damn you," he muttered. "Damn and damn." He knew all too well that his father was up at the house, sound asleep, knocked out by the hard cider that he must have started on right after Silas left for the dance. "Am I supposed to take care of him, be his boss?" Silas said angrily. Again, the nearest cows stretched their necks to look at him. Peace and quiet, he told himself again, silently vowing that when he had a place of his own, he'd run it proper, provide for his family and keep his house, barn and fields in fine shape. With Sarah? Could he take care of her proper? He reckoned. That thought smoothed the wrinkle on his brow.

Milking his way along the line, he discovered that some cows had been milked. Their udders weren't bulging, and two were lying down, legs sprawled, contentedly chewing their cuds. Not for the first time, he thought about that. Old food getting masticated again. He shuddered. Good for cows, mebbe, but anytime he'd had food come back up, it didn't warrant chewing it again.

Satisfied that he'd relieved the pressure on the unmilked cows, he glanced at one of the high windows behind the animals and realized he really had made good time. It was nowhere near light yet. He made his way to the house with two pails of milk, pausing in the cellar to place them in the icebox. He glanced toward the back of the cellar where his mother stored her beets and carrots and where his father made the vinegar and hard cider. The dipper was there, and he walked over, picked it up and drew a half cup of cider. He looked at it a minute, wondering what the magic of this brown liquid was, that it pulled his father away from duties. He took a long swallow and instantly spit it out. It was strong, not sweet like cider, had a little burn to it. He shook his head and laughed, remembering how he and a young cousin had got into the barrel at the other boy's house. They dared each other to drink, and both choked, then went outside to roll on the ground and laugh and pretend they were drunk. He shook his head, set the dipper down and tiptoed upstairs, skipping the pesky third tread that had been protesting footsteps for years. He stopped in the kitchen for a drink of water to get the bad taste out of his mouth, then went upstairs quietly. He stripped off his pants and shirt and crawled into bed, knowing he would have to sleep fast. Dawn was not far away. He s'posed Sarah had been asleep for hours. A small smile crossed his face as he thought about her head on a pillow, and he dropped off.

A couple of hours later, he roused to the sound of his mother lifting stove lids and adding sticks to the fire. Not enough, he thought, with a huge yawn, but he knew he couldn't just roll over. He had a notion about what had gone wrong with the barn chores and milking the night before, but he also knew it wouldn't be worth talking about. It was likely his father had hit the hard cider before four in the afternoon and passed out amid the end-of-day work. How he'd gotten himself to the house and to the bed where he was snoring when Silas went by his parents' door, he didn't know. His mother would no doubt enlighten him when she got around to it. He sighed, pulled on a shirt and overalls, put the clothes he'd worn the day before into the cupboard and went down to the kitchen.

"Father's in the barn," his mother said without turning away from the stove where she was stirring oatmeal in a red enamel kettle. "Want syrup on yours?"

"Please," he answered, getting the message that she wasn't about to tell him anything. He took a seat at the table across from Minnie, who had set the bear he won at the fair on the empty chair. He took a tablespoon from the tumbler and poured syrup over the oatmeal his mother had served up in a blue and white bowl, which made him smile. His mother wasn't an elegant woman, he knew, but she had certain niceties she liked to observe. One was that nothing as dull looking as oatmeal – which she never ate herself – should be served in a white bowl. "Surroundings," she would say if anyone commented. "Pale, washed-out food needs surroundings."

He dug in, hurrying a little because he was worrying about the cows and wondering if Sarah's mother served boiled potatoes on white plates. He planned to ask her and smiled thinking about the look she might give him. His mind moved on to hoping he was wrong about Father. Maybe he was sick and needed help to get through the morning. But as he swallowed the oatmeal, he knew better. It was, once more, the drink.

"Thanks," he said to his mother, who still hadn't really looked at him. In the back room, he pulled on his barn jacket and boots and headed for the barn. He found his father mucking out the trough behind the cows and getting ready to milk. His greeting was met with a grunt. Another parent not looking at him.

Silas picked up a shiny milk pail, a damp, ragged towel and one of the three-legged stools and headed for Matilda, always the first cow to be milked. He set the stool down, wiped the cow's udders with the towel and settled himself to milk, quickly moving into the familiar rhythm. Almost immediately, one of the barn cats appeared, putting her front paws right on his left boot and giving a loud meow. He pointed a tit at her and squirted warm milk into her open mouth. She instantly disappeared.

When he had pretty much drained Matilda's udder, he stood, set the pail aside and took another. On to Zilpha. He approached her carefully, since she was a little unpredictable and had sometimes been accurate enough with her right rear foot to land a bruising blow to his leg or, worse, hit the pail when it was half full. Today, perhaps because she was one of the cows he had milked in the wee hours, she just glanced around at him and stood perfectly still. By this time, his father had finished the cleaning up and run the wheelbarrow up the plank to the manure pile outside the barn. Out of the corner of his eye, Silas saw his father get a pail and stool and move to the next cow where he leaned his head heavily against the animal's flank. Head probably breaking in two, Silas thought. Certainly, his eyes were as red as winter flannels. He sighed, drained the last drops from Zilpha and moved on. And so they went, alternating animals and without a word between them.

When they were finished, they carried their pails to the milk room, and set them in the cooler. After a second breakfast, Silas would leave to deliver containers of milk to the general store and hope it was worth enough to wipe out the running tab there. He wished he could shut off his father's right to that tab, but that would hurt his mother, too. And that, he realized, would affect the dinner table. He went upstairs, looking forward to a cup of coffee and a few pieces of toast but wondering about setting with his silent father. He need not have worried. His sister chattered and chattered, so much that he stopped listening and let his mind drift back to the night before. It already seemed as if it had all happened weeks back, but he was all too aware that he had known Sarah for less than a month. He started figuring on how he could manage another visit. At least her father had said he could call, but he wasn't certain how to arrange that. He'd think on it. Mebbe ask his mother. She must have been courted once upon a time. Hard to see it, but it must have happened.

He glanced at his father, who was shoveling food in his usual way, staring at his plate as if he were afraid it would move. Silas spread a little more crabapple jelly on his last piece of toast, licked his knife and looked to see if his mother had noticed this breach of etiquette. Etiquette. He was back to the courting question. He finished his toast and took his plate to the kitchen. When his mother followed him, asking if he needed anything else, he shook his head and then whispered, "If a boy has permission to call on a girl, does he just show up at the door?"

Jane Hibbard burst out laughing. "Nothing ventured, nothing gained," she said.

"What does that mean exactly, Mother?" Silas asked, trying not to sound annoyed. He really did want the answer to his question, but his mother liked her adages and proverbs and quotations so much that she rarely resisted tossing them about. And never seemed to run out.

"It means he walks up to the door when it's not mealtime and raps on it and then talks to whomever opens it and hopes he doesn't get run off the place," she said, still chuckling. "And you tell your mother who this boy and this girl are."

Silas felt his face reddening. "What difference does it make?" he asked, wishing he hadn't started this.

"Depends if you're Myles Standish or John Alden, I reckon," his mother said.

That made Silas laugh and reluctantly say, "I'd be John.

But there ain't no Myles."

"Isn't any," Jane Hibbard said, frowning. "Far as you know."

"And I won't get run off. Her father said I could call on her. She didn't let on that anyone else had been given permission."

"Well, then," his mother said, obviously nonplussed about so much going on that she didn't know about. "Well, then," she said again. "If you're hankering to see this young lady, Sunday afternoon would be proper. And easy. The menfolk will be snoozing after dinner, and no one's obliged to work." She looked straight at him then and asked, "Is she pretty?"

"Quite."

"Then keep in mind that you can't judge a book by its cover," Jane Hibbard said. She chuckled again and added, "Pages inside could be blank." She turned toward the stove where the tea kettle was bubbling away and said over her shoulder, "Mighty nice of you to fix up the cows in the middle of the night."

Silas headed for the stairs to change into his Sunday best, wondering how his mother knew about the late milking and how she put on such a cheery front when she had to know, and know why. His father must have been at the cider again. But he wasn't about to ask. He'd had more conversation just now than he cared about having, and the only comforting thing was that he'd gotten away without disclosing Sarah's name. And that Minnie hadn't been there to ask questions. Sometimes a seven-year-old was a pest. But he knew his mother would be carefully questioning all the ladies at church today. He'd take the buggy for the long ride to Eastborough, holding out hope that Sarah would like to take a ride with him.

CHAPTER SIX

Sarah was running her fingers around the inside of the mashed potato pot, trying to get it clean. The kerosene lamp by her mother's chair didn't provide enough light to wash dishes, but supper had been late, the pot had been left soaking while they went dancing, and here she was, scrubbing away as if she were blind. No, no, she thought. I don't ever want to be blind. "Not ever," she said aloud.

"What's that?" her mother asked. "Not ever what?"

"Be blind," Sarah answered, thinking how dumb that sounded.

"Course not," her mother answered, as if she often thought the same thing. She went back to reading the weekly newspaper that had arrived that morning, the chair creaking whenever she rocked.

Sarah rinsed the dishes in the basin of clear water and emptied that into the bucket under the sink. Her mother would use it to water plants outside, despite the fact that they might get a little soap along with a drink. No brown leaves so she supposed no harm was being done. She wondered if dousing potato plants might get rid of some of those pesky orange bugs. They were so ugly, and Father would be sending her to pick them off by hand and drop them in a bucket with a little kerosene in the bottom. "Dreadful," she said aloud with a little shiver and figured

SARAH MEETS SILAS

she was better off with blindness. Why was it that boys so delighted in bugs and girls shrank away? She'd have to ask Silas if he liked picking up snakes and potato bugs and grasshoppers. The thought of him made her smile and sigh at the same time.

"Soon's you're done there," her mother's voice came, "we'd better get to bed. Chores to do early so's we can get to church on time. Nell's invited some young fellow for Sunday dinner, so you can leave the potato pot out. Reckon I can start a chicken before church, add some potatoes and carrots and give him a decent meal. She seemed quite fussed when she said she'd asked him, but I gather she just met him at the dance?"

"Indeed, Mother," Sarah said, starting to laugh. "Did he ask Father if he could call on Nell, or is he merely a hungry acquaintance?"

"No idea," Emma said. "But she pinked right up when she announced he was coming."

That made Sarah laugh again. "She pulled him into a special grand march. I don't think she ever seen – saw – him before."

Emma nodded approval at the correction and then sighed, thinking about Nell. "She's impulsive, too impulsive. We shall see what we shall see. Time for bed." She set the paper aside, stood and headed for the stairs. Over her shoulder she said, "Come Monday, see to some holey socks in the basket. Any that's too bad, just pair them up as best you can. Hard to darn a hole that already has a hole."

Sarah laughed. "With their boots on, men won't know whether socks match or don't. And they get dressed in near dark anyway." To herself she said, "Work's never done, never finished." Sighing again, she dried the plates and put them away, then dried the flatware and glasses, which went back to the table for breakfast. The mending basket did look pretty heaped up. If that was all socks, there'd be a reckoning before dawn one day. She started for the stairs, candle in hand, and wondered who darned Silas's socks. At least she wouldn't have to darn tomorrow – no sewing on the Lord's Day. Sometimes she liked rules.

She was still thinking about rules when she pulled the thin quilt up and dropped her head on the flat pillow. The ropes that held her mattress creaked a little as she turned on her side. What, she wondered, were the rules of young men calling on young women. Would she and Silas have to sit in the front room and talk about whether it might rain in the morning? Would they sit on a sofa or on straight chairs on opposite sides of the room? Would they take a walk? Would she suggest things to do, like that silly business of looking at white flowers, or was that up to him? Or her father? Or mother? If they were in the front room, Nell would be busying herself close to the door, straining her ears to listen. She wriggled deeper into the covers and decided to stop thinking about it. What would happen would happen. She fell asleep hoping they'd just take a walk. By themselves. And he might take her hand.

She woke before dawn, feeling a little more tired than usual. Too many thoughts after going to bed, she decided, as she pulled the chamber pot out from under the bed and squatted. Too many dreams. She dressed quickly, putting on a skirt and shirtwaist her mother would find acceptable for church. She buttoned her shoes, poured water into the bowl on her washstand and washed her face and hands. She brushed her hair quickly, aware that her mother was already moving around in the kitchen. She hurried down to help.

As she expected, her mother looked her up and down and then nodded approval. Sarah usually took this inspection for granted, but today it irritated her, scratching her brain like sandpaper. She knew what to wear and when. Her mother, after all, had taught her. If I ever have children, she thought, I'll let them get dressed as they please and hope for the best. Then her mother smiled and held out a bowl of oatmeal. It wasn't her favorite, so she felt that odd grating in her mind again. But she took it to the dining room, found a spoon in the tumbler and sat down to eat. She wondered what Silas was doing. Did he have oatmeal for breakfast, too?

Silas, in fact, was two and a half miles into his journey, suddenly calculating that he might arrive well before Sunday dinner, which would confound everyone, himself included. What if they were still in church? Ah, he thought. That would be better, really, much better than barging in if allowed in – while everyone around a dining room table looks up and stares. In the churchyard, he could offer Sarah a buggy ride home. "Yes," he shouted, the sound making Dolly pause to look over her shoulder before settling into the rutted road. Silas felt his eyelids droop, pulled them up, felt them insist on closing. He'd just let them have their way, just for a minute, what his mother called a catnap, for some reason. He nodded off.

A half hour later, Dolly took the buggy through a puddle and across a deep rut, jostling Silas awake. He looked around, saw they hadn't strayed from the right road, rubbed his eyes and checked to see if his trousers were splashed with mud. For the thousandth time, he wished he had a watch. He'd have to choose the right minute and ask his father if he could borrow his if he was going to be making long trips where time mattered. Most of his sense of time so far had depended on dawn, dusk and his growling stomach. He chuckled. His stomach was keeping time right now, raising a new question. What if he arrived at Sunday dinner time? Perhaps he'd have to hide in the woods for an hour or two. Permission to call on a man's daughter was more complicated than he'd thought. What if they invited him to dinner? Sarah seemed special. Her mother might set a fancier table than his mother did. Or not. He decided not to trouble himself with more what-ifs. What will come, will come, as his mother frequently reminded him. Sure as the wagon follows the horse, she'd say. He'd better pay attention to the road and keep the horse out of puddles.

Must be within a half mile or so, Silas thought, as the horse trotted steadily on. But the road was in rough shape here, making his stomach roil as if he'd had baked beans for supper. Or mebbe he was getting cold feet about arriving in Eastborough. Something, mebbe everything, was making him as skittish as a cow on a plank bridge. He leaned back, took a deep breath, let it out in a long sigh and told himself to settle down. He'd better spend a penny so he'd be saved asking Sarah about facilities. He pulled Dolly to a stop, threw the reins over her head and ducked behind a large oak by the side of the road. Back in the buggy, he relaxed and told himself that whatever was going to happen was pretty much out of his control.

Not long after that he saw the church spire up ahead. And then he was near enough to hear the bell. Trying to ignore his grumbling belly, he thought about how he'd always wanted to pull on one of those big ropes and make the bell ring. He wondered if Sarah had any pull – oh, good one, he thought – with the sexton or deacon or whoever had the bell-ringing task. Mebbe bell ringing would be a safe subject if he found himself at the Sherman dinner table. Never could tell what might set somebody off, and these were all strangers. Even Sarah.

He pulled up short of the church just as the door opened and the pastor stepped out. People followed, dressed in their Sunday best, and each stopped to shake the minister's hand. He seemed to have something different to say to each one. Then Sarah stepped out. A shiver down his spine took him by surprise; she looked downright beautiful. He threw Dolly's reins over a nearby hitching post and slowly walked toward the group, now buzzing with conversation. The week's gossip, he knew. His mother loved those after-church talks about the week's events and, again, he was pleased she didn't have Sarah's name. It would have been a welcome novelty in a town where the chatterers could make a goat having twins into a story.

He was dithering about, wondering what to do next when Sarah turned and saw him. He watched as she excused herself from two other girls and made her way toward him, smiling. He reached in his pocket and pulled out a freshly ironed handkerchief and proffered it when she was close. That made her laugh.

"All this way because I might be in tears?" she asked.

"Like to be prepared," he answered. And then they just stood, looking at each other.

"Say something," she said, suddenly shy.

"Glad to see you," he said. He paused, and she realized he was blushing a little. "Woke up thinking about you," he said a little gruffly.

"Me, too. Um, of you, I meant."

To his surprise, she reached out her hand and started to pull him toward the knot of people around her parents. Gratefully, he saw Nell and that young man named Jason Harris in the group, along with Sarah's father, the man who scoffed at baldness. He saw her mother look up, spot them, frown and then smile and come toward them.

She saw Sarah pulling me along by the hand, Silas thought, trying to extricate his fingers. But Sarah held on and, her face flushed, introduced him to her mother, Mrs. Sherman. Nell joined them almost immediately, grinning.

"How grand to see you again, Silas Hibbard," Nell said. Turning to her mother, she added, "We met Silas at the square dance. He's from Grafton."

Emma Sherman prided herself on not being surprised by anything. She extended her gloved hand to Silas, who realized he had forgotten his gloves in the buggy and would be offering her a hand roughened by farm work. But Emma was looking at his face, not his hand, so they shook and smiled.

"You've come a far piece," she said. "Perhaps you would join us for Sunday dinner?"

"Be more than pleased," Silas answered, thinking things were moving faster than he was ready for. Whatever would he say at dinner? "Breakfast seems like history right now." That made everyone chuckle, and Sarah's father stepped forward to shake his hand.

"All the way from Grafton and missed church?" he commented. "I reckon you're right on time for the best part of Sunday."

"John!" Emma's mother exclaimed. "It's a day of rest because of church. It's the Lord's Day."

"W'aal, not all rest," Sarah's father answered. "Cows to be milked, manure to be shoveled, pastor to be listened to."

"John!" his wife remonstrated. "This young man will be getting the wrong idea about us."

"Dinner, too," John answered, unperturbed. "That's not a rest. Best meal of the week." He glanced at Silas, his eyes taking less than a second to inspect him head to toe, and said, "Right day to come, young man."

"I'll ride with Silas," Sarah said, wondering if she were being "forward," something young ladies were never supposed to be. "Just to show him the way," she added quickly to make her wish seem practical. And to stop her father from talking, she thought. As Silas nodded, Nell chimed in to proclaim that she and Jason would join them, if the buggy had room. "Plenty," he answered quickly, hoping no one noticed how his smile slipped away when he realized he would not have a moment alone with this pretty girl he'd come to see. "This way," he said, pleased that he'd taken the time to dust the buggy seats just before he entered the town. At the buggy, he gestured for Nell and Jason to get in the second seat – he was not about to sacrifice having Sarah sit next to him just because, most times, men rode together with the womenfolk behind them. Jason, he realized, had seen right through that and actually gave him a wink as he hitched his horse behind the buggy, helped Nell up to the seat and climbed in after her.

Didn't Sarah squeeze his hand more than need be while he helped her in? He hoped so. He unhitched Dolly, she backed away from the post, and Sarah indicated where they should go. All was silent for a few minutes, mostly because Nell wanted to hear what her sister and her beau were saying. But she never was one to be quiet for long, so she started to talk to Jason about the weather, telling him her father was like a scientist about whether it would rain or shine the next day. "Never gets caught with a lot of hay lying on the ground for a thunderstorm," she said.

"Reckon I better get in touch when I'm about to put a project out to dry," Jason said.

"Project?" Nell asked, instantly interested in finding out more about this handsome young man who was actually going to be at their Sunday dinner table.

"Furniture," Jason answered. "I raise chickens and milk a few cows, but mostly I'm in wood and furniture. Have to put a piece outside now and then to dry the finish. But only in the shade."

Up front, Sarah smiled. Now she could talk to Silas. Nell was busy with Jason and seemed quite enthralled. She tapped Silas on the arm and asked, "Was the sun up when you arrived home?" The minute the question was out of her mouth, she decided it was a silly thing to ask. But you could never take back escaped words. She was grateful when Silas answered in a serious tone, as if it were important. He told her the night for him, the sleeping part, was dang short.

"I woke up wondering when I could see you again," he said, watching her without turning his head. "And I realized I'd just have to take the bull by the horns, get the chores done and head out."

"Bull by the horns?" she laughed. "I have no horns and little relationship to bulls."

That made him chuckle. "When you live with my mother, you hear a dozen things a day like that," he said. "They get stored in your head and pop out now and then. My teacher got annoyed proper when I used one in an essay."

"I had a teacher like that, too," Sarah said. "She says we should 'invent our own images.'"

"And do you?" Silas wanted to know.

"Sometimes."

They were quiet, and then Sarah said, "Silent as a cloud."

"What's that?"

"Inventing an image," Sarah laughed. "Turn right at the next road."

"Sometimes," Silas said, "clouds rumble."

"Inventions aren't always perfect," Sarah countered, thinking this was one of the oddest conversations she'd ever had with anyone. And very nice, too. She did love words, and most of her family laughed at her when she used a new one. "High falutin" they called her.

Silas made the turn and put the reins in his left hand, reaching for Sarah's gloved one with his right. Fearing she'd pull away, he gave it a squeeze, let go and put his hand back on his leg. He was startled and pleased when she pulled off her glove and pulled his hand into her lap. Behind her, Sarah heard Nell's small gasp and realized her sister was watching her like a hawk. Was that a cliché? She giggled at her own silliness, and Silas squeezed her hand, his fingers moving over hers. It was grand to be here at this moment, but he was still worried about sitting down for dinner. What if they had fish? He'd eat trout right out of the stream, but otherwise? No. How he hated that dried cod his mother mixed up with top milk and other things and served over a biscuit. It just smelled like dead fish to him.

He was surprised at the size of Sarah's house, which had two floors, a colonial look and a handsome barn behind. He saw pastures stretching out behind and realized how shabby his parents' home was with paint peeling on barn and house, fence posts tilted and a discarded hay rake rusting near the barn. He'd like to have a place like this someday, and he was all but certain he'd like to share it with Sarah. He'd not like her to work as hard as his mother did, but perhaps that was the way it was. He tried to look sideways at her and realized she was staring at him.

"What?" he said, immediately thinking that was stupid.

"Glad to welcome you here," she said quickly, putting his hand back on his leg. "You'll find a hitching post just there," she added, pointing. "And we should get your horse some water. Do you want her outside or in a stall, and is she likely hungry?"

"Yes."

"All that, I reckon. But you didn't say about the stall."

"Loose in the pasture acceptable?"

"Yes." And she laughed.

Grateful to have something to do, Silas jumped down and reached a hand up to Sarah, while Jason did the same for Nell. The girls immediately started for the house, lifting their skirts to avoid any dew in the grass. The two men looked at each other and then stood by the buggy, watching the girls hurry along.

"Beautiful girls," Jason said, shaking his head. "Just beautiful."

"Yes, twice," Silas answered. "You been here for dinner before?"

"Nope."

"My first time, too. Not bad for a square dance." And both of them laughed and went to unharness Dolly. Jason swung the gate open, and the horses walked through, looked around, then put their heads down and broke into a run. Silas watched for a minute, noticed that the water trough near the gate was full and turned toward the house.

"What'll we talk about in there?" Jason said from behind him.

Silas stopped on the stone step beside a small pump and pushed out enough water to rinse his hands. "No notion," he said. "Jest hopin' I won't spill on my shirt."

Jason chuckled as he washed up. "And I'm thinking Nell will talk – she does run on -- and no one will notice if I'm tongue-tied or use the wrong fork."

"Think they're fancy?" Silas asked.

"Reckon not, but if there be a lot of glass and flatware on the table, I may have to go check the horses. Just as a kindness. To the horses."

They were both grinning as they entered the dining room and saw a table nicely set for Sunday dinner but not fancy. Sarah's mother indicated chairs for each, putting Sarah beside Jason and Nell beside Silas, causing both of her daughters to pout for an instant before they realized they were across from the man they wanted to look at. Nell did look, straight at Jason until he smiled. Sarah had her eyes on the freshly ironed tablecloth, all too aware that Silas was staring at her. John Sherman automatically raised a hand for silence, although the room was already strangely silent. They all bowed their heads while he said grace. That done, the girls got up and went to the kitchen, returning with a platter of chicken and potatoes and a bowl of carrots. They set the food down by John, who had a stack of plates in front of him, and he immediately started to carve the chicken.

"Great hen, this one," he remarked and was immediately shushed by his wife.

"Don't go on, please," she said.

"Sorry. Might I say that this chicken has no local connections."

All four young people grinned, and Emma Sherman lips tightened into a thin line, but she said no more. The plates started around the table, and Emma passed the gravy.

"I do love a rich gravy," Silas said, keeping his shirt in mind while ladling it on his chicken and potatoes and surprised that his voice sounded quite normal. This might be a piece of cake, as his mother would say. "My mother always puts in a little of the water from the vegetables of the day."

"As do I," Emma Sherman said, wondering if this young man knew how to cook as well as charm her daughter. "And scrapings from the pan."

So we're going to talk about gravy, Nell thought, and decided to plunge in. "Not too much flour," she added.

"But enough," Sarah said, finally making her vocal chords work.

"Gravy," John Sherman pronounced, "is one of the best things about Sunday. That and the nap that will likely overtake me within the hour. But I just want to eat it, while you young men give me an idea of what your day is. Not Sunday. The real day."

Silas nodded at Jason, who immediately plunged into how he had to rise early and get the cows and chickens taken care of before sun-up and breakfast. Once he et, he said, he went to his workshop to build furniture, which he hoped one day would be his living. He also put in considerable time at a sawmill to put food on his table.

"Live alone?" John Sherman asked.

"Yep. Rent my place from a farmer who took a room in town when he got sick of taking care of cows and chickens before sun-up."

"What kind of chickens?" Nell's father said, his eyes focused on this young man who seemed to have put a spell on his daughter after one Virginia reel.

"The farmer had plain old Rhode Island Reds," Jason said, thinking he would rather talk about gravy. "I kept 'em, but I do like a touch of class in the henhouse. Added some Chinese birds last year."

John Sherman's eyebrows shot up, and he leaned forward, not noticing that Nell had pushed back her chair and headed for the kitchen. "They lay, or are they just good-looking?" he wanted to know.

"Eggs and looks, sir," Jason said.

"You sell or eat one now and then?" Mr. Sherman persisted.

"Yes, sir. A fat Sunday chicken always brings in a little change. But not the Chinese ones."

"Usually the womenfolk take care of the chickens," Nell's father said. But he leaned back in his chair and glanced toward his wife. He must have gone too far with this probing, he thought. Her lips were a bit tight.

But John Sherman wasn't finished. He turned to Silas and asked, "Whose progeny are you?"

"Caleb and Jane Hibbard, if you mean my parents, sir. We farm in Grafton."

Emma's brows were tight now, too. She was anxious about her husband offending these young men with his prying. Then she smiled, a small smile, and asked if anyone was ready for pie. And Nell came back to the table.

Silence fell while everyone ate the juicy apple pie, Silas once again thinking about his shirt and noticing that Mrs. Sherman had served the pie on glass plates. He'd never seen such before. When forks rested around the table, John Sherman tipped his chair back, put his napkin back in the silver ring that bore his initial and closed his eyes. Emma waved her hand in his direction, put her finger to her lips and quietly stood, as did the rest. They left the dining room, plates in hand, with as little noise as quite a few adults could make.

In the kitchen, Sarah took plates from Silas and Jason and said, "You could set on the porch if you're staying awhile," Sarah said, "while Nell and I see to the dishes."

"Nonsense," Emma said. "You all get out to the porch. I'll get a start on the dishes." When they reached the porch, they found John Sherman, wide awake. He wanted to know more about chickens and asked how Jason fattened his up if he needed a little income and wanted to sell one or two.

"Don't mind sharing the secret, sir, since you're nowhere near my market," Jason answered.

Mr. Sherman chuckled and Jason went on, "Found what your wife would call a receipt in this journal I get from Boston. You heat up some cornmeal until it turns into kind of a dough, boil some old potatoes, mix it up and feed it. Couple times a week I scald some sour milk and feed the curd."

"Heavens!" John Sherman exclaimed. "You just tell the other chickens to hold off on that special feed?"

"Have to separate them, actually," Jason said. "But they plump up nice in a short time. And the ladies love them. Certainly helps cut down my tab at the store. Speaking of the biddies, I'd better get home. Chores waiting." Silas immediately said he was sorry, but he also needed to get on home for milking.

"I'll walk with you to the barn," Nell said. "You coming, Sarah?" And she held onto Jason's hand as she headed down the porch steps.

Silas looked at Sarah. "Shall I take your hand, too?" he asked in a mischievous voice. "I think I have permission, but I'll wager friend Jason isn't even asking. I wouldn't want you to trip on a stick or a stone."

Sarah laughed and held out her hand. "Nell is always so sudden," she said.

"And you're not," Silas said. "But I do have your father's blessing."

"Sort of," she said in a teasing voice. "Only sort of." And they followed Jason and Nell to the barn holding hands. Emma, watching from the kitchen window, smiled. Two nice young men. It must have been quite a square dance.

CHAPTER SEVEN

"Envy you the short trip," Silas said to Jason as he harnessed his horse.

"'Pears you might get a mite closer soon," Jason answered with a chuckle, watching the color rise on Sarah's cheeks.

Silas shrugged and busied himself with harness and hitches. Without answering, he turned to Sarah and said, "Perhaps I will hear from you again soon?"

"Mebbe so," she said, keeping her eyes on the ground. Then she smiled and added with a glance at Nell, "But I have no more ironing to do."

When Nell laughed, Jason muttered, "Sisters. It's like a conspiracy." But when he looked at Silas, he realized this exchange wasn't a mystery to him.

Silas boarded his buggy grinning, waved to Sarah and was gone before anyone could explain. Torn between wishing he'd at least touched her arm again and not wanting any displays in front of her sister, Sarah watched until Silas was out of sight. She went back to the house without saying goodbye to Jason but watched from the window as Nell moved closer to her new beau and took both his hands in hers. Sarah turned away, thinking it was not seemly for her to watch. As she headed for the stairs, she wondered if Jason had kissed her sister. If only she were as brave as Nell.

For his part, Silas realized he'd rarely felt so good. Either his hands were sending some new current through the reins or Dolly had liked her feed at the Sherman barn because she was trotting like the youngster she wasn't. He'd be home long before dark at this pace, in time to give the herd a dipperful of chopped carrots before milking. Didn't know why a cow liked carrots, but it provided a use for the knobby ones his mother did not like. As he passed the general store in Eastborough, he pulled Dolly up and looked for any kind of sign about future square dances. Nothing. But he did see notice of another country fair opening in two days in West Bridge. He wondered if the farmers would take their makeshift games there and whether that small dark boy had recovered from the blow to his head. Might be worth stopping by, just to see. Odd that the bleeding boy had led to the ironing of a handkerchief. He was still angry about the first and thankful for the second. Life was strange – his mother probably had one of those tired sayings for that, but it didn't come to mind at the moment.

Four days later, Silas loaded his father's wagon with hay and set out to deliver it to a farmer who'd had a sparse crop the year before. He never calculated what the return per hour was on such a mission because his father figured it was mostly a boy's time, not worth much. A little cash would be welcome, and it sometimes irritated Silas to have his worth dismissed that way, but not today. West Bridge was only a tad off his route, and once the hay was delivered, he would go to this fair and see if that colored boy was still at work. Give him something to talk about next time he saw Sarah. He supposed, he thought with a grin, the lad's worth wasn't valued much either, despite the coins collected by the man who'd rigged up the game.

Silas fingered the two coins in the pocket of his overalls. He'd been well paid for getting those sheets of glass to Mr. Goodnow, and he'd never told his mother how much he'd gotten. He'd put a couple of dollars in the small basket she kept on a pantry shelf and exchanged the rest for two Grant dollars. Pure gold they were, and he carried them with him for two reasons. He liked to look at them now and then, and he didn't want anyone at home to know about them. He sauntered through the fairgrounds, stopping to admire the sheep and the pigs and eventually getting to the corner where games were being played.

Ah, the baseball-throwing game was there and, indeed, the pickaninny – his brain braked sharply and backed up, knocking out that word and putting in Negro, mostly to please his mother – was poking his head through the hole in the deer hide and dodging the balls thrown at him. They were using wooden balls this time, he noted, and as the boy's head turned, he saw he still wore a sizable bandage on the side of his head. It was dirty, but to Silas's relief, it looked as if it were attached by someone who knew what he was doing. So at least the child had been to a doctor. He hoped no infection had set in.

He moved a little closer. The boy didn't seem to be afraid, and he hadn't lost his response time. Thwack. Thwack. Thwack. One ball after another hit the stretched leather and fell off. Then one sailed toward the target, the boy's face disappeared, and the ball fired into the hole and landed with a thud. He is amazing, Silas thought. Hoping the child would heal soon, he turned to go and saw the left-hander from Ripton strolling toward him. The star pitcher. A pitcher with a cruel streak, worse, a mean, venomous streak. He paused. With a friend on either side, Lefty Wheeler was buying three tickets from the man beside the game. He was given six balls and gave two to each of his friends.

Silas was riveted to his spot. Was it going to happen again? One of the friends threw first, thwack, thwack. Two misses. The second friend went to the line and sent his first ball right into the hole, but the boy's face was gone in time. They all groaned, and Silas felt a sense of relief, wondering at the same time why he cared. The young man, tall and awkward, frowned, wound up and threw again. This time, the ball sailed over the makeshift target into the field beyond. Now it was Lefty's turn. Silas moved closer, and Lefty glanced toward him with a grin.

"Have to show 'em how it's done," he said.

Silas glanced toward the boy and saw his eyes go wide. He remembers, he thought. He's terrified that he can't do it. A few feet away, the ticket man's eyes narrowed, and he took a step toward the boys. He, too, was remembering.

"Go, Lefty," one of the friends said. Lefty wound up to fire the first ball, and Silas dove for his legs, knocking the pitcher to the ground and landing on top of him. "Judas priest," the pitcher yelled. Silas heard the shout and was almost immediately crushed when both of Lefty's friends piled on. As the four rolled and wrestled, the ticket man bellowed, "Help! Fight!" and nearby fair-goers swarmed toward the fracas like bees seeking their queen. No one stepped in to stop it. "Help!" the ticket man yelled again, and a constable wearing a badge on his overalls broke through and tried to separate the four.

"Need a hand here," he said, looking at the circle of people around him. And three men stepped forward to stop the fight.

"Sit 'em down," the constable ordered. When they were seated, Lefty and his friends glaring at Silas, he asked what had happened. Lefty immediately said he was just playing the game and this other person he didn't know had come flying at him.

"He spoiled my shot, wasted my money," Lefty said, while his friends nodded in agreement.

"And you?" the constable said looking at Silas. "You attacked him?"

Silas paused. He was about to create an enemy. He didn't think he'd ever had one, not on the street, not on the playground at school. He thought of Sarah, sitting on that rock at the other fair, crying her eyes out.

"He's," and he pointed to Lefty, "the one who hit the boy in the head at another fair. And he did it by cheating. That's why the child is bandaged, could have been killed. I just happened by and saw that he was going to do it again, so I knocked him down."

"True?" the constable asked Lefty.

"Not true. I'm no cheater."

"True," said the ticket man, "absolutely true."

"How?" asked the constable.

"He throws one ball with his right hand and follows immediately with his left. It throws off the child's timing. He was badly hurt last time," Silas said. "Lefty's a star pitcher, a southpaw."

The constable turned to Lefty's friends and asked, each word clipping the next, "Is that true?"

They fidgeted but did not speak.

"Sunday School true?" the constable insisted.

The blond friend pushed back the hair on his forehead. He was starting to sweat. "True he's a southpaw," he muttered.

Silent until now, the crowd that circled the group began to murmur, some pointing at the boy with the bandage, who seemed frozen in place. The ticket man spoke again. "I remember him," he said, pointing at Lefty. "At another fair, two weeks back. Threw right, then left, so quick I barely saw the ball leave his hand. Had to get stitches for the boy with the doc in town. Cost me a pretty penny."

"You are how old?" the constable asked Lefty.

"Fifteen," he said, his head down.

"Speak up."

"I have fifteen years."

"Sir."

"Fifteen, sir."

"Stand up."

Lefty stood. His hands were shaking, and a small trickle of blood was seeping through his pants leg. Must have hit a stone when he went down, Silas thought, realizing that he felt a little shaky himself. He'd not meant to hurt anyone. But he was still angry.

"You," the constable said, "are to leave the fairgrounds this minute and never approach this ticket man again, no matter where he brings his act and his pickaninny."

Negro, Silas thought. But he didn't even whisper it.

"And if I hear of that bullet, left-handed pitch hitting a batter anywhere in the county, I will be after you on criminal charges. You understand?"

"Yep."

"What's that?"

"Yes. Yes, sir."

The constable looked at the other two boys who were still slumped on the ground. "Get him out of my sight," he told them. They scrambled up, motioned to Lefty and walked quickly through a sudden opening in the wall of spectators. Silas didn't move.

Then the constable looked his way and said gruffly, "First time it's been my duty to approve an assault. But don't make a habit of it." He turned away and went to talk with the ticket man, who had two tickets in his hand and was on his way to offer them to Silas free. He wasn't a man to miss a chance to whip this crowd into buying more. But Silas shook his head and walked off, still thinking about how angry he'd been for that split second. And how exhilarated he felt now. He wondered what Sarah would think, and then he remembered how she had sobbed when the Negro boy had been hurt. He'd wager one of the coins in his pocket that she didn't say "pickaninny." He grinned suddenly, thinking what might have happened if he had corrected that piece of vocabulary. Might have lost the crowd. He'd better get on home. He wasn't making any money here.

Little did Sarah know, as she went to change her clothes, that Silas was attacking the young man who had upset her so. She was musing, as she put on her house dress and old shoes, about how often good things happened just when you were thinking everything was dreadful. Fright, tears and then a handkerchief. He'd already been to dinner with her family, and she hadn't pursued him. She was certain as snow in winter that Nell had somehow seen Jason after the dance and before the Sunday dinner. She wished she had Nell's nerve.

In the kitchen, Nell was already getting leftover chicken out of the icebox for supper. Sarah knew dinner would have been prepared at the noon hour, but it looked as if they would have more than biscuits and honey for supper. Without any chatter, she set the table for the meal, making sure the tumbler with the large spoons was in place. She was grateful her father hadn't insisted on one of those spoons for Sunday dinner when the guests were there. He often wanted a soup spoon to scrape every last bit of gravy or food off his plate. Her mother told her to be happy he didn't lick it. She shuddered. She couldn't even imagine that. She did like things to be nice. She wondered if Silas's mother was fussy about such things. When would she see him again? Hmm. What would Nell do? And suddenly she knew. She'd give a note to young Henry at the store, and he'd keep it until Silas happened by. Sooner or later, he'd be there. She knew it.

After supper, she asked her mother for paper and whether they had ink for the pen. Emma said they likely did, and she fetched paper, pen and ink from the little desk in the front room. Sarah excused herself and went upstairs. She didn't want Nell reading over her shoulder or asking questions. Quickly, she wrote that another square dance would be held in a fortnight in the next town. Perhaps you will see fit to attend, she wrote, thinking that sounded very hoity-toity. But it was there in ink, and paper was dear, so she signed her name, folded the note and put it in the drawer of her dresser. She'd take it to town as soon as she finished her chores in the morning.

CHAPTER EIGHT

"Shall I mow today?" Silas asked his father as they perched on their stools for the morning milking.

"Spit on your finger and see how the wind blows," his father answered, without lifting his head from the cow's flank.

Silas wanted to scoff at the spit method of predicting the unpredictable New England weather. But it worked as often as not, so he'd do exactly that when the milking was done. He moved on to the next cow and sighed. This was Zilpha, a master – or was it mistress – of kicking the milk bucket. And having an uncanny instinct about when it was near half full. He set the milk pail aside and took down a thick rope from a peg on the wall, lifting Zilpha's back right leg and putting it through the loop on the rope. The other end was attached to the wall, the rope now stretched tight. He tested it. Zilpha would be able to kick back but not forward. He placed the stool, ready to milk her and had to smile. Turning her big head, she had given him a look. He'd spoiled her day.

Heading up for breakfast, Silas paused to try the spit trick, then told his father which way the wind was moving. Turned out he'd be mowing, hoping for at least three days without rain so the hay could dry and be stored. Their small field had a good crop of rowen this year, and Silas always thought it was the tastiest hay for the cows and horses. Not that he'd ever eaten any, he reminded himself. Without any more talk, they tucked into a breakfast of oatmeal, eggs, toast and strong coffee. He always hoped for the sizzle and smell of bacon or sausage but knew both were dear and required cash at the store.

Miles away, Sarah Sherman was flipping sausage patties in a cast iron spider with one hand and stirring half a dozen eggs with the other. Father had been to Mr. Fuller's farm the day before and paid the farmer cash for the newly prepared sausage and a slab of bacon. She wished they could have this every day, but she knew it wasn't always available. Besides, Mr. Fuller always wanted cash money.

"Your father will need you this forenoon on the tedder," her mother said, coming in from feeding the chickens, ready to sit down for breakfast. Sarah sighed, and her mother frowned. "Did you have something else in mind?" she asked. "He figures sun will get to the hay 'bout eleven o'clock. Hopes it'll be dry late tomorrow or next day."

"No, ma'am," Sarah answered quickly. "What else could there be?" Eating quickly, she started upstairs to change into her oldest skirt and thickest shirtwaist. She hated the way hay scratched her skin, so she would choose to be uncomfortably hot, not itchy, and wear the same outfit until haying was done. If the good weather held, she knew she'd be even more uncomfortable tomorrow. Once the limp green grass had turned crispy in the sun, she knew she'd be atop the wagon, stomping each forkful as her father and Nell tossed them up. She knew her father liked the way she loaded the wagon so the weight didn't shift and send the whole load into a heap on the ground. She liked telling them where the next forkful should go, once the four corners were covered. It was always hot, sticky work, followed by more hot, sticky work when the wagon was backed into the barn and unloaded into the hay mow. At least Nell was the one who had to clamber into the mow and push the hay back. She sighed, wiped her forehead with her arm and wished Saturday weren't so far off. No bathtub until then. Perhaps Nell would go for a swim after supper. Otherwise, she'd itch for days.

By the time she was ready, she was scolding herself for being selfish. They always needed to gather the hay as quickly as possible. Beating the weather, her father always said. No doubt Silas was haying today, too. That idea put a smile on her face before she reached the kitchen and saw a look of relief cross her mother's face. Her mother gestured for her to take a seat and sat facing her.

"I know your father gave young Silas permission to call on you, but I must ask you what your feelings are about the matter. He seems very intent on courting you, and he seems, so far, to be a fine young man."

Sarah felt her face getting red. She didn't want to talk about Silas, but she reckoned she had to – right now. Hesitating, she said, "He is fine. I like him."

"But you haven't met his parents. You haven't seen where they live and how they live."

"Does it matter, Mother? About how his parents run a farm and keep house?"

"If you have even the smallest notion to put your future in his hands, the answer is yes."

My future, Sarah thought. My future in his hands. I am beginning to think I'd like that immensely. A whole lot. She looked at her mother calmly and said, "Then I'd better get him to invite me to Sunday dinner." And then, unable to resist, she added, "Nell seems to know how to do such things on very short acquaintance."

She immediately worried that she'd gone too far, but her mother just chuckled and took her basket of eggs to the pantry. Sarah cleaned up the dishes and went to the back hall to pull on boots. Then she went to find her father who asked her to hitch one of the horses to the tedder. Minutes later, she was in the middle of the field, going round and round, guiding the horse and looking back to watch the row of little forks flick the hay in the air. This must be tedding, she thought, since it's a tedder. But why isn't it a tosser? She bypassed a spot where someone had tied a white rag to a stick, getting the message to stay away but wondering why. In less than two hours, she had covered the field twice, so she headed toward the barn where her father was waiting.

"Pretty good sun," he said as she pulled up. "Mebbe we can get that bunch raked this afternoon and get ahead of any storm that has an eye on spoiling my plans."

"Oh, Father," Sarah said, "You are such a pessimist."

"Goes with farming, Sarah. You can ask your Silas about that."

"Not my Silas, Father," Sarah said, but the color of her face put the lie to her words.

"Take my word for it, Sarah. He's planning on it. And appears to be a fine fellow."

Sarah didn't answer. She couldn't believe how often she'd felt speechless since she'd accepted that handkerchief. First one parent, then the other. But she just nodded to her father and went up to the house to see about the noon meal. The sun was nearly overhead, and she'd been so fussed over the mention of Silas that she'd forgotten to ask about the white rag in the field. Well, it would provide conversation at the table, which was sometimes a very silent meal. So different from Sundays, she thought. Was that because no one was working his head off on Sunday? She wondered if Wednesday could be eliminated and Sunday repeated. She laughed. You are demented, she told herself. But she did like the sound of "your Silas." Would he be?

Haying time, Emma had to serve the noon meal more than once. She sometimes felt getting in the hay ate up all their lives. So Father and the hired hand, plus Nell and Sarah, arrived anytime between 12 and 2. In winter, she and her daughters often had supper before the men came in from the milking, but somehow, she didn't know how, on most summer evenings, they all ate together when it was nearly dusk. It gives the dining room a little time to cool down, her mother would say. Emma didn't like the noon meal spread out so. Sometimes it seemed to run right into supper.

"They'll be right along," Sarah said, coming into the kitchen. "Hay's drying well. I'll be on the rake this afternoon, and Father says if we don't have a heavy dew, we'll bring first of it in late tomorrow." Emma nodded, pointed to Sarah's seat and, as soon as she sat down, placed a plate of meat, boiled potatoes and green beans in front of her. Sarah made short work of her dinner and went back to the field where she hitched a horse to her father's new dump rake and set off to where she'd run the tedder that morning. She knew Mr. Chandler still hand-raked his fields and called this rake "new-fangled." Sarah realized she pretty much liked new-fangled. The old wooden rakes were so wide and made her back hurt.

She doubled up her long skirt so the metal seat wouldn't burn and set off. After the horse went a short way, the hay rolling up under the curved rake behind her, she pulled the lever and released the hay. She was proud of being able to go about the same distance before the next dump, then turned at the end of the field and started back. Now she had to put the next piles in line with the first ones. Windrows. She wondered where that strange word had come from. It was a long process, and she again skirted the cut grass around the white rag. Had to ask about that. As she finished the last row, she looked back. Her windrows were straight. She turned the horse toward the barn, where her father would take care of the horse and rake. She did need a swim.

At the house, haying done for the moment, and a red-hot sun dipping behind the trees, the family gathered to eat a cold supper of sliced pot roast, Dutch cheese and potato salad. "Sailor's delight," John Sherman said as he started to eat. "Farmer's delight."

When everyone was settled, Sarah said, "Father, I took the horse around a stick with a white rag this morning."

"Just as well," her father answered, a slight smile crossing his face.

Sarah gave a small sigh and received a frown from her mother. But Nell wasn't about to leave the subject there and asked, "What was it for, Father? Does it mark hidden treasure?"

"Ground bees," John Sherman said. "Forgot to warn you."

"Good thing she went around," Mother said, turning her frown on her husband.

"Yep," John said. "Glad we saw it before we turned it inside out. Those bees can swarm all over a horse and send the poor animal running. Sorry, Emma, I should have warned her. But the message came through. If it had been Nell, she'd have stopped the horse and knelt down to poke around. But not Sarah."

Emma nodded, but her frown didn't ease. Sarah looked at Nell to see if she was insulted, but her sister was grinning and remarked after a pause, "You-all know me too well." Sarah decided she might have just received a compliment, but she wasn't sure. The talk stopped abruptly when everyone heard wheels crunch on the gravel behind the house.

"See who that is, Nell," John Sherman said, and Nell eagerly jumped up and looked out the window. "Young Henry Goodnow," she said. "And he's coming 'round to the side door."

"Then open it," her father advised, "and invite him in. Hard to imagine what brings him here this time of day."

She opened the door, and Henry handed her an envelope. "It's for Miss Sarah," he said, "and I reckoned with all the haying and what-not she might not be in town any time soon." He reddened and added, "My father said I should fetch it now." He turned to go, and John Sherman called out, "Come on in, boy, and set with us. Shouldn't come all this way without getting a cup of tea and mebbe a piece of Emma's pie."

So Henry left his hat by the door and took a seat, while Nell glanced at the envelope and handed it to Sarah with raised eyebrows. Sarah felt her face getting hot. It was Silas's handwriting. Everyone looked at her, but she tucked the envelope in her pocket and said, "I'll get the pie, Nell, if you'll put the kettle on."

At the door to the kitchen, Nell jabbed her with her elbow and hissed, "You're not going to share, are you?"

Bumping her sister with her hip, Sarah said, "It's addressed to me. Mother says letters and notes are private."

"Gr-r-r-r," was the only reply, as Nell checked the fire, then pulled the kettle to the front of the stove. It was already humming, so it wouldn't take long to boil. The teapot was in its usual place, keeping warm on a shelf above the cooking space. She filled two tea strainers and hung them in the pot. She noticed that Sarah was in the dining room with the blueberry pie and plates, and she gave a little sigh. Why should she expect a letter to be shared anyway? She'd had word from Jason and had told no one.

As soon as they finished the pie and tea, everyone pushed back their chairs, Father to finish up in the barn, the women to take care of the dishes. No catnaps today – never in haying season. "Dawn to sunset takes a good while," John Sherman said. "Wears a man out." And everyone laughed because he said the same thing every day when hay was on the ground. Today, he looked at Sarah and added, "Best tend to your correspondence," and she nodded and fled to the stairs.

Silas's note took away all the tired and the simmering resentment about the fact that she could have been badly stung. He had seen notice of the square dance on Saturday and wasn't just asking to dance with her. He wanted to fetch her. "Escort," he said. Unless she sent word to the contrary, he would come by with his buggy a half hour before the fiddler tuned up. She could tear up her letter and stop worrying about it. She paused on the stairs – would they let her go with Silas? Father had said he could call. Did that include going off in a buggy? She hoped so. She went to find her mother and ask.

CHAPTER NINE

Sarah and Nell never stayed mad at each other for long and were chattering away about what they would wear to the Saturday dance when Father came by. He had already given permission for Sarah to go with Silas, so the sisters were startled when he interrupted to say, "Be a good idea for Nell to ride along with you and Silas, Sarah. We old folks can take the small buggy."

Sarah was startled by this news and glanced at Nell to see if it had been her idea. Nell shook her head and was about to speak when their mother came up behind her husband and said, "I think not, John. Nell will ride with us, and Sarah will go with her beau. You gave that young man permission to call on her, and it doesn't include Nell, sir."

Now, everyone was startled. Emma Sherman rarely spoke up on family questions, but here she was, doing exactly that. Relief flooded over Sarah. She didn't know why she so craved that private time in the buggy with Silas, but she'd thought of little else while guiding the horse through the hayfields that week. She looked to her father and saw him smile.

"So be it," he said.

The week plodded on like their oldest horse, but Saturday came, and Nell and Sarah boiled water and filled the galvanized tub in the kitchen, after serving notice on their father that the house was off limits for an hour. They took turns in the tub, then called up the stairs to their mother so she could take her turn. She would dip out some of the water and add more hot. Then she'd do the same for John. They all liked to bathe before him because, as they occasionally teased him, he was always plain dirty.

Upstairs they dressed in everything except their skirts. They could certainly get out supper and eat with their father in their shirtwaists and petticoats. The square dance skirts were so full, they were a nuisance, catching on doorways and billowing up at the table. After supper, they finished dressing and went downstairs to wait in the parlor.

"No running out to get in your young man's buggy," Mother announced as she appeared in a blue skirt, ivory shirtwaist and a blue bow at her neck.

"What do you mean?" Sarah asked.

"It's proper for a young man to call at the door for a lady," Emma answered. Frowning slightly, she added, "I expect you to be properly behaved for the entire evening and remember how you've been brought up."

"Don't worry about Sarah, Ma. She's always proper," Nell said. It came out in a way that made it sound like something deserving punishment. "You do look lovely, Ma," she added.

Sarah laughed. "Proper it is," she said, wondering if she'd like improper better.

"And please don't call me Ma," Emma added.

At the sound of wheels on gravel, they all turned to the window. It was Silas, reining in his horse and jumping down from the buggy. He threw the reins over Dolly's head and ran up the steps to knock on the door.

"Very handsome," Nell said with a sigh. She motioned Sarah to wait and went to open the door to invite Silas in. Sarah realized she was blushing, and her hands were shaking. She knotted them behind her back and managed to squeak out a greeting. Silas spoke to Emma and Nell, then nodded to Sarah.

"I see you are ready," he said, his voice steadier than his heartbeat. "Shall we?"

"Yes," Sarah said, taking her summer shawl off the sofa. She'd stopped shaking, but her hands felt damp, so she hesitated when Silas held out his hand. The evening was pleasantly cool, but she felt as if it were 100 degrees. But she took his hand, told her mother and a grinning Nell she'd see them at the dance. She hoped she wouldn't trip on the porch stairs. You are a ninny, she told herself.

She could tell Silas had cleaned Dolly's harness and shined the metal parts. The buggy had the nose-pleasing aroma of scented soap, and she felt her eyes tear up when she saw a small bunch of buttercups tied to the arm bar with twine. She had worried that this was more special to her than to Silas, and now she knew. It was just plain special. She sat, tried to gather up her skirt to make room for Silas and smiled at him as he hopped onto the seat.

Putting the reins in his left hand and giving Dolly the word, he reached for her left and gripped it so hard she was afraid a bone or two would crack. At least she wasn't shaking anymore. She pulled her shawl around her shoulders and laughed at herself for worrying whether her hair would escape its pins on the way to town hall.

"Welcome," Silas said. "I am so glad to see you, so happy you let me escort me tonight. I was afraid your father and mother would think it unseemly for us to set off by ourselves when we barely know each other."

"I think I know quite a good amount about you," Sarah said, wondering again if she was being forward. Everyone made it sound like "being forward" was a church-like sin. She reckoned if she was guilty, she liked it. That made her smile again.

His fingers were running over hers again, and then stopped on her index finger. "What I know is you take up more than your share of the seat. What I don't know is where this scar came from."

"It's old," Sarah said. "And it was all Nell's fault," she added, thinking she'd never dared say that out loud before. "I was ten. We were told to sharpen Father's scythe on the grindstone, and I was holding and she was turning the handle. She stopped and said I needed to try it out and should test it with my finger to see if we were done. Success? Sharp scythe and bleeding finger."

Silas frowned. "Did the doctor come?"

"We never call the doctor. Mother stuck a needle in the fire to clean it, threaded it with her finest quilting thread and took a tiny stitch to pull it together. Then she put ice on it. The bleeding stopped."

"And no infection?"

"Nothing. But it hurt, and it was Nell's fault."

Silas lightly stroked the scar again, and again, Sarah felt

a little shiver run down her spine. Trying to find something meaningless to talk about, she asked, "How's the haying?"

"Hayed for hours," Silas answered. "Were you out there? Did you make ginger milk for your father? So hot."

"I ran the tedder after he mowed and the rake in the afternoon," she said. "Narrowly avoided stirring up a nest of ground bees. And after the ginger milk he put me on top of the wagon to stomp. I am," she said, relieved to be on safer ground, "the best stomper in the county."

"You see? Another thing I didn't know about you."

"Good at stowing it away in the mow, too."

"Ah, all kinds of skills. You'll make a marvelous wife for some lucky man one day."

Sarah choked down a gasp, thinking haying hadn't proved the perfect neutral subject. But before she had to answer, they had pulled into the yard of the town hall and Silas was asking if he should let her off at the door or take care of Dolly first.

"I'll go with you," Sarah said, torn between being anxious about being alone and overwhelmed by walking in with this young man. Tongues would wag, she knew. The town's gossips liked nothing better than getting to the square dances early so they wouldn't miss a thing.

So he helped her down and turned horse and buggy over to the boy from the livery stable who'd give Dolly water and a little hay for a small payment. Silas never liked tying his horse up to a post and leaving her. Then they walked to the town hall, not holding hands. Outside the door, to Sarah's dismay, a bunch of young men had congregated, and she felt all of their eyes – at two each, would it be at least 30 – on her and Silas. Two or three called howdy to Silas, who nodded back and as they went by, Sarah heard one mutter, "some pumpkins," which made Silas laugh until he realized she was mortified.

"It's a compliment," he said, taking her hand. "And it wasn't meant for me. It was for the prettiest girl arriving at the dance. They just wish they were me."

"Glad they're not," Sarah said a little sharply. "I like compliments as much as anyone, but I think they're a little rude."

Silas just laughed again, unable to stop enjoying having a girl for this dance and none of them did. As they moved on, one of the young men called after them, "Heard what you did to Lefty!" Uh-oh, Silas thought, I can't even hope she missed that. Sure enough, as they took a seat in a row of chairs lining the room, Sarah said, "What was that about Lefty?"

Before he could answer, a tall man stopped in front of them and held out his hand to Silas. "Talk around town is that you gave that southpaw his comeuppance, young man. Proud to hear it. Been too big for his boots for some time." Silas stood, accepted the handshake, and thanked the man.

"Perhaps you'll tell me now?" Sarah asked, already figuring he couldn't have done anything bad. That was Mr. Leonard who'd shaken his hand, and he was one of the nicest teachers at the school.

"Stopped him from hitting the Negro boy again," Silas said, so quietly that she had to lean toward him to hear.

"What?" Sarah said. "Where did you see him?"

"Been on the lookout since the day we met," Silas said. "Wasn't at the first fair but last week I came across him buying tickets for two baseballs. The little boy was right there, dirty bandage on his head, his eyes darting back and forth from Lefty to the boss ticket man. The ticket man didn't move, so I did." He fell silent, shuffling his feet and looking at the floor.

"More," Sarah said. "What does that mean – move?"

"Decked him, just before he threw," Silas said, looking right at her. Briefly, he wondered if she was going to get up and walk away, but instead she pressed her shoulder close to his and said, "I want to know the whole story. Did he get hurt?"

"No blood," Silas said, remembering there'd actually been a bit of blood. "But it wasn't friendly. Someone yelled 'fight' soon as we hit the ground, so people circled 'round, and a constable came to bust it up. I was still angry, but I wasn't aching for a fistfight. I was a little worried about what his friends might do. Maybe I could finish the story later when we're not in the middle of a hall?"

Dying to hear more and also thinking how much Nell was going to like this, Sarah nodded. The room was filling, and the fiddler was plinking strings and tuning his fiddle. Suddenly, he gave a shout: "Time for a circle!" Townspeople were on their feet, quickly realizing one circle wouldn't be enough, so a smaller one formed inside the first one.

"Grand right and left," the fiddler called. "Inside circle clockwise, outside counterclockwise." And after a moment of confusion, the circles began to move. "Funny," Silas said, "that some folks have to pause and figure which way the clock goes." That made Sarah laugh as she left him to circle the hall. Decked him, she thought. Who'd have dreamed

Silas would seek out that nasty baseball player? She saw Silas coming toward her then and realized that nasty pitcher was the reason they'd met. Her mother was right. Silver linings. And then his hand was in hers, and they smiled and moved past each other.

Sarah felt as if her feet had wings that night. She was whirled and twirled by Silas and by her corners, and she had a happy feeling that was quite new to her. It made her smile even more when she spied Nell in a square with that handsome Jason and hoped he had sought her out, not the other way around. She worried about being forward herself, but she knew Nell was. Which reminded her, as she executed a do-si-do, that she needed to get an invitation to Silas's house for Sunday dinner. Should she propose church? No, that would wake up every tongue in his village. Then the Red River square ended, and Silas took her hand and appeared to steer her toward the refreshment table where gray-haired ladies were ladling iced tea. But he veered off suddenly, and she found herself at the back door of the town hall and then outside in the cool summer air.

"Thought we should check on Mrs. What's-Her-Name's flowers," he said without a hint of a smile.

"Mrs. Wellspeak," Sarah said, and across the road they went to look at white flowers. As they stood looking at the gardens, Sarah wondered if he was going to kiss her. She shivered at the thought and felt his arm go around her.

"Chilly?" he asked, wondering how anyone could be cold on a warm night like this. "Need to go in?"

"No, sir, thank you very much. You can see tonight how the almost full moon makes her garden shine in the dark."

"I do see," Silas said solemnly, tightening his arm around her waist and wondering if he could kiss her. Or, if not now, when. The arm was enough, he decided, reveling in the fact that she hadn't pulled away. She was an odd combination of open and shy. He sighed, and she turned toward him.

"Shouldn't you also see that it's time to be telling me the story – all of the story – about you attacking a star pitcher in the middle of the fairgrounds?" she asked.

Silas sighed again. The town's grapevine had given him away. So he told her about how his anger had boiled right up when he saw Lefty buy three tickets and how he dived for the pitcher's legs before he could throw the ball. He told about the crowd and the constable and how the ticket man had told the story just right.

"So the constable didn't haul me off to jail," he finished.

"Did he take Lefty to jail?"

"Didn't. Told us all to behave and told Lefty not to appear at another fair this year."

"How did the Negro boy look?"

"Scared, when he saw Lefty. Knew him right off. Constable called the child a pickaninny. My ma wouldn't tolerate that talk."

"As I wouldn't," Sarah said. "Would you?"

"Reckon not," he said, sounding a little impatient.

"Did I say something wrong?" Sarah asked.

"What's wrong is I came out here hoping to be alone with you, and the pitcher and the boy are making it quite a crowd."

"So, what else should we talk about?"

"I'd just like to put my arms around you," he said, the words bursting out before he could stop them. To his surprise, she stepped close and circled his waist with hers. "Ah," he said, pulling her close. Yep, open but shy. Burying her head on my shoulder. Can't kiss her if I can't see her. But he stood still, she stood still, and the moon inched along above them.

"The fiddle is playing," he said after a minute or two. "We'd better get in some more dancing."

She mumbled something he couldn't hear, pulled away and linked her arm in his. They walked back to the noise of the town hall, eyes on the gravel path, silent and smiling.

"Nice flowers," Silas said, and Sarah giggled.

Two dances later, the caller announced a grand march, and everyone fell into place while the fiddler struck up the "Battle Hymn of the Republic," and by the time the townspeople were eight across, they had begun to stomp their feet and sing along. Sarah grinned at Silas and joined in the singing and stamping, thinking that her father would be worrying about the timbers cracking beneath the floor. Then it was over, and the happy dancers jammed the path to the front door. Sarah saw Nell, arm-in-arm with Jason, and wondered if they had kissed. Would Nell tell? How do you kiss anyway, she thought. It's not like a peck on auntie's cheek.

Then they were in the buggy, and Sarah settled her shawl around her shoulders. Pretty much inside her own thoughts, she didn't notice when Silas missed the fork leading to the Sherman farm. When she started to look around, she realized they were going the wrong way, and she said, "Silas, you missed the turn."

"Not really," he said, not looking at her.

"Really," she said.

"I didn't miss it," he said quietly. "I wasn't ready to take it."

"What does that mean?"

"It means it's a lovely evening for a boy to drive with a girl in the moonlight."

Glad he couldn't see her cheeks flame, Sarah said, "A boy and a girl?" And wished she hadn't.

But he answered quickly, "This boy and his girl." And wondered if he'd gone too far. His mother surely hadn't been much help with what to do next.

"I like the sound of that," she said, so low that he barely caught the words, but he transferred the reins into his left hand, put the right around her shoulders and felt that now familiar tremor run through his body as she moved closer and put her head on his shoulder again.

The horse trotted on, and neither talked. Sarah had closed her eyes, enjoying the smell of Silas's jacket and the rhythm of the horse's hoofs. But she sat up straight when that rhythm turned into a clack, clack, clack and then stopped. They had halted. She looked around. It was quite dark, and she realized they were inside the covered bridge that led across the creek to the next town. Moonbeams shot through the slats on one side of the bridge, and Silas turned toward her.

"Tradition," he said and, lifting her chin, kissed her so gently it was like being brushed with a feather.

"We have many traditions in our family, but I never heard of this one," Sarah said, trying to sound more calm than she felt. "Where did you …" But before she could go any further, Silas kissed her again, less gently, then tilted her head back to look at her.

"I hope I haven't overstepped any …" But now she stopped him in mid-sentence, holding his cheeks in her hands and kissing him, her soft lips staying on his chapped ones much longer than he had kissed her.

"How do you know how to do that?" he demanded, breaking away.

"I don't," she said. "I've never done it before." Oh, dear, she thought. He'll think he's my first beau.

"Neither have I," Silas said, laughing. "I think we should practice again before another buggy comes along." And so they did. Until it struck Silas that everyone else would be home from the dance by now.

"Have to get on," he said, picking up the reins. "You'll be the last one home."

"Or maybe Nell," she said, and when she heard herself laugh too long, she knew Nell would say she was giddy.

He spoke to the horse, and she continued across the bridge without hesitating. Silas mentally thanked her for standing still awhile and not balking the way many horses did on bridges. He was not going to tell Sarah he'd come along earlier in the week to see whether Dolly would willingly cross the bridge. Might upset her to know the long way home wasn't spur of the moment.

"Where did he come from?" Sarah said suddenly, interrupting his thoughts.

"Who?"

"The little boy with the dressing."

"Asking around, I found out he came up from Georgia, mebbe only four or five years old at the time, after his folks were set free. The ticket man lives several miles out of town and has let the family live in a hunting shack at the back of his farm."

Sarah shivered. "Former slaves," she said.

"Yep."

"Which town?"

"I reckon that's still Eastborough out there, but I don't exactly know."

Sarah was silent, remembering how men in the family refused to talk about their days with the Union Army. Except they all told about Negroes following them as they trekked back to their homes in the North. They had been given their freedom and lost their homes, she thought. Shacks, prob'bly.

"So he has family," she said.

"Yep." He took her hand and said, "He'll be all right. Made it from Georgia, didn't he?"

She smiled and startled him by asking, "When will you call again?"

He'd better get used to these odd starts and stops of talk, he thought. Her mind flitted all over the place. Not flitted. Changed direction. He thought about the kiss and answered, "Like you to meet my mother. Wa'al, my father too, but my ma mostly. Could collect you of a Sunday for church in my town and Sunday dinner at the farm?"

Sarah almost gasped. She'd been working up to suggest such a thing but hadn't figured the right way to do it. And now it was there, as plain as knives and forks on the table. But her mischievous side came to the fore, and she asked, "Does permission to call include permission to carry off?"

"Yep."

"You have lots of yeps tonight."

"Feeling a little speechless," he answered, squeezing her hand and guiding Dolly into the Sherman yard. Coming to a stop, he jumped out and gave her a hand getting down. But her foot caught on the hem of her skirt, and she toppled toward him, ending up in his arms. He steadied her and released her. She turned toward the house without speaking but looked back when she reached the steps.

"I had a very nice time," she said primly and disappeared into the darkened house.

Silas did not move for about three ticks of a clock and then he climbed up, clucked to the horse and tried to go slowly so he wouldn't wake the whole dang family, but Dolly sensed it was time to go home and took off around the house and back onto the road with considerable jangle and clatter. Once they were well on their way, Silas relaxed on the seat and closed his eyes. He hoped to doze off but instead kept thinking about those sweet kisses and about Sarah saying she'd had a nice time. But she didn't say she'd come for Sunday dinner. She didn't say she wouldn't, he reminded himself. And sometimes her conversation jumped around like a startled rabbit. He had been there beside her, all warm and excited about her allowing a kiss, and she'd asked about the injured Negro boy. He realized he was glad she cared, but why then?

He nodded off, and Dolly took him home, rounding into the driveway only a couple of hours ahead of milking time. He roused himself, took care of the horse and considered that lending a girl a handkerchief had turned out to be more than he'd bargained for. As he trudged toward the house, he grinned. Mebbe quite a bargain.

CHAPTER TEN

AT HER HOUSE, Sarah opened and closed the door as quietly as she could. A kerosene lamp gave off a yellow light in the kitchen, but otherwise the house seemed dark and still. She sank into her father's rocker near the stove, a wide smile breaking across her face. He had kissed her. She had kissed him. She tried to think about what it all meant, but she couldn't get past how much she'd enjoyed that kiss. She hoped he didn't remember that she'd said it was her first. That was mortifying. She'd wager a nickel that Nell had kissed Jason more than once. And mebbe others.

She pulled herself out of the chair, snuffed the lamp and tiptoed up the stairs to the room she shared with Nell. She removed her clothes, folding them on the table rather than opening the wardrobe door, discovered that Nell had laid out her nightgown on the bed, so she silently slipped into it. She wondered what time it was as she climbed into bed and snugged the coverlet around her shoulders. She jumped as Nell's voice came out of the dark.

"Not asleep, Sarah. Waiting for you. Did he kiss you? Did he take you to the bridge? You are really late. Mother and Father went to bed muttering about 'that young man.'"

"Yes and yes," Sarah said. "I can't think what to think."

Nell snorted. "You must have wanted him to," she whispered. "You did, didn't you?"

"Yes," Sarah whispered back. "What I also want is that I don't want to talk about it." And she turned toward the wall and closed her eyes, then sat up again and asked, "How did you know about the bridge?" Across the room, Nell murmured, "Hmmm," and then smiled in the dark. Sister Sarah was smitten and afraid to say so. She immediately thought about Jason. He had appeared to like being with her most of the evening, but he'd asked her where her father's wagon was when it was time to go home. Sarah had been kissed, she thought. She was certainly going to inquire about what brought that on so she could proceed differently in the future. Unless Jason never wanted to see her again. She stared at the ceiling for a long time, even though it was too dark for her to see it, and finally fell into a restless sleep. After noting that Sarah had trundled instantly into the Land of Nod.

The sisters woke at exactly the same time the next morning, and each sat up straight immediately. They looked at each other, and Nell said, "So why did you come home with Silas and Jason helped me into Father's wagon?"

"Silas escorted me to the dance," Sarah said, saucily. "It would have been improper for him not to see me home."

Nell scowled, having no answer for this piece of truth, and got up, pulling up the bedclothes on her side and yanking the chamber pot out from under the bed. Sarah heard the sound of her sister making water and thought about being escorted. Right to the covered bridge, where she had to kiss him, didn't she, in the name of tradition? And because I wanted to, she admitted, wondering how long Nell would wait to ask about that again. And I'd like to see the bridge again today, she thought, and turned away so Nell wouldn't see her face reddening at the very notion. Silas would have been at the barn for more than an hour by now, and she hoped he was thinking of her while he did his chores. And thinking of bridges.

But she didn't want to share that with Nell so she said, instead, "Silas had a row with Lefty Wheeler."

"What? Where? When?" Nell was totally distracted from the kissing now.

"He went looking for him at fairs," Sarah said, thinking she both liked the idea of his doing that and thought it was simply awful that Silas wanted to hit somebody.

"Oh, dear God," Nell said sitting down on the bed abruptly. "He's in love with you."

"I am starting to hope so, Nell," Sarah said, sitting next to her. "But don't you want to hear the story?"

Nell nodded. She was seeing her sister as she'd never seen her before. Quickly, because they were expected in the kitchen, Sarah told the story and Nell gasped more than once and then said, "He got his deserts. Silas did good." Sarah said, "Well," and they both laughed. As they went down the stairs, Sarah went back to thinking about bridges.

Somewhat sleepy, Silas had the covered bridge on his mind, too. He leaned his head against the flank of the last unmilked cow and folded his fingers around two of her teats. The milk spurted into the pail, and he sighed. The night's sleep had been a mite short. Not only because he was so late getting home but because his mind had been racing. He wondered if he should have counted Sarahs instead of sheep. Perhaps so. Sheep pretty much looked all alike, as you counted, but not Sarah. He saw Sarah with skirt flying at the square dance, Sarah's face barely visible as they stared at white flowers, Sarah bawling on a rock at the fair. And Sarah, barely visible again in the dark of the covered bridge. He shivered, which made his fingers twitch, and the cow stretched her head around to look at him. It's all right, he told her. Well, it was and it wasn't. He couldn't stop thinking about that first kiss, how warm her mouth was, and how she'd returned it. He'd never loved anyone outside the family before. He reckoned what he felt for his parents was love, although he'd never really thought about it. But that was love with obligation. Sure as eggs is eggs, he didn't owe Sarah love. Just wanted to give it to her.

"You gonna milk that cow all day?" Silas's father's voice snarled from behind him. "Cow's got a right to rest."

Startled out of his dreaming, Silas nearly spilled the pail, but he hung on and looked up with a grin. "Bit tired from gallivanting, I expect," he said calmly.

"Can't let the night paint the day," Caleb Hibbard said, scowling at his son. His red-rimmed eyes told Silas that his father had been at the drink again and prob'bly had a bad night himself. He stood, picked up the milking stool, stored it and headed for the house with the milk. No point getting into it – or anything else – when his father was red-eyed. He wanted to invite Sarah for Sunday dinner, but what if his father was in what Silas thought of as his cider mood. He figured he'd have to risk it. He wanted to kiss her again. He wanted to marry her. When that thought floated into his mind, he nearly lost the milk bucket again.

"Judas Priest! You are stumbling around like a two-year-old," came his father's voice again. "What on earth has come over you?"

Silas didn't answer. Inside, breakfast was ready, and he was relieved to see his father bend to his food. He reached for a spoon from the tumbler on the table and started in on the bowl of oatmeal. Mebbe when he was dressed for church he'd ask his mother about Sarah coming for dinner the following Sunday. He'd have to risk whatever Saturday night might bring on for his father, who nearly always found a reason to go to the cellar after supper of a Saturday. Might take the cruet with him, he'd say, so's to refill it from the vinegar barrel, which happened to be right next to the smaller barrel where cider was allowed to ferment. When he was only seven, Silas had sneaked down after him, watched as Caleb took a dipper from the top shelf, turned the spigot and filled it. Even then, he was pretty sure he was looking at a secret, so he never said a word except to ask his mother what was in the little barrel. "Medicine," she'd said, not looking at him, "case we need it."

Three hours later in the churchyard, his father moved off to speak to a neighbor, and Silas asked his mother whether his new friend Sarah could come for dinner the following Sunday. Jane Hibbard grabbed his arm and stopped in the middle of the path.

"It's like that, is it?" she said a little sharply. "Reckon I should have guessed. It's been plain as the nose on your face."

"What has, Ma?"

"You've taken a fancy to that Eastborough girl."

"Reckon I have, Ma," Silas said.

"Time we got acquainted, I reckon. We'll kill a chicken." She called to Minnie who was meandering off and started walking again, Silas at her side wondering whether this was a welcome or quite the opposite. Only one way to find out, he figured. He'd get young Henry to deliver another note.

CHAPTER ELEVEN

"You soft on this boy?" John Sherman had demanded when Sarah told her parents about Silas's note. She hadn't answered until he said, "Sarah?" And she told him Silas had been very kind to her and she liked going to square dances with him. Her father had said something that sounded like, "Hmmph," and gone back to eating his apple pie. Her mother had said nothing, except to tell her to wear her Sunday best and mind her manners. She did, nearly always, mind her mother, but mind her manners? They didn't speak, far as she knew. And now she was sitting beside Silas in his buggy again, and she couldn't think of a thing to say. She hadn't seen him for days, and she was struggling to talk. What on earth is the matter with me, she thought.

"Mighty quiet today, Miss Sarah," he said, glancing down at her.

"Can't think of a subject for conversation," she said stiffly and nearly gasped as the dreadful sound of that echoed in her mind's ear.

"You could ask how far it is to my house," he said teasingly.

"How far?"

"A few miles."

Sarah started to laugh. "That went nowhere," she said. "I think I'll say you were in my thoughts every day since the square dance."

"That seems like a good idea," Silas said, his grin widening.

"What?"

"Telling me I was in your thoughts."

"What?"

"So tell me." He shifted the reins to his left hand and dropped his right arm around her shoulders. "Tell me about those thoughts."

Sarah looked up then and realized he was laughing at her. She felt a little fussed, and she wasn't quite sure what he was expecting. So she leaned into his shoulder and whispered, "I mostly remembered the moonlight coming through the slats at the covered bridge." Silas drew on the reins, and Dolly stopped in the middle of the road. He kissed the top of Sarah's head, then lifted her chin and kissed her on the mouth.

"For the next fortnight," he said, "you can remember sun shining in the middle of the road."

"Will it be that long before I see you again?" Sarah asked, her face now scarlet but her eyes shining.

"Depends how you do at dinner, I reckon."

"Oh, lordie me," Sarah said, relieved when Silas flicked the reins and the buggy moved on. Both were silent for a long stretch, and Dolly turned into the next road, very narrow and lined on both sides with wild blackberry branches that grabbed at the buggy wheels. Leaving a trail of dust, the buggy took another turn onto a road where grass grew between the well-traveled ruts. And then Sarah saw the house and barn and felt her stomach do a flip-flop. They were there. The house was smaller than hers, with a porch running the length of the front and around on one end.

She could see two gaps where spindles were missing, and the porch sagged at the far end. They pulled around back, where a stand of sunflowers stood near the back steps.

"Will you go to the barn with me, or shall I take you in now and then take care of the horse?"

"The barn," Sarah said, thinking about what on earth she'd say if left alone for ten minutes with Silas's father and mother. So he unhitched Dolly and put her in her stall with water and grain, then took Sarah's hand and walked toward the house.

"I'm pretty nervous about this, too," he said, "but I'd consider it helpful if you could look a touch less grim. This isn't an execution, just an introduction. Do you need a handkerchief?"

That made Sarah laugh, and she squeezed his hand and put on a smile just as Silas's mother opened the door.

"Ma, this is Sarah Sherman," Silas began.

"Reckoned it would be," Jane Hibbard interrupted. "Right pleased to meet the person responsible for Silas waking up the cows in the middle of the night. But he does haul out of bed at dawn anyway, so it's no trouble."

"Ma," Silas began again.

"Sorry, Miss Sarah. Warn't tryin' to upset you. Pleasure to welcome you. I confess to having a hankering to meet a young lady who could pull Silas away from his horse and his carrying business to go dancing." Silas sighed, and his mother held the door for them to come in. She pointed to the parlor door and said, "Mr. Hibbard will be down soon's he gets cleaned up. You set, and I'll get the dinner on."

From the corner of her eye, Sarah could see that Silas

was standing very still, so she walked across the parlor and asked about a framed picture on the wall. When he said nothing, she said, gently, "Silas?"

"Are you upset?" he asked.

"Certainly not."

"What you're looking at is either art or a grim notion. My grandmother's hair, made into a wreath, which would be all right if she'd cut it off and twisted it into a circle. But they cut it after she died, so it's a memorial. Seems dreadful. And a little spooky."

To his surprise, Sarah grinned mischievously. "You might consider that it would have been even more cruel to cut it when she was alive. Her crowning glory, as it was. What's grisly, I think, is covering a dead face with plaster and turning it into a sculpture. Better to sit five minutes for a photograph."

Silas laughed then. "I never know where your thoughts are going to go," he said.

"Is that troubling?"

"Charming," he said, just as his mother appeared and beckoned them to the dining room. Sarah realized her thoughts were hardly leaping about at the moment. She was just worried about whether she'd like Mrs. Hibbard's cooking and whether her stomach, which felt a mite queasy, would be all right. Then Silas introduced his father, a pleasant looking, red-faced man who was pulling on a suit coat over his suspenders. She suspected that was in her honor. She relaxed a little when everyone bowed their heads, and a familiar grace was said. And the roasted chicken in front of Silas's father was brown and crusty, with bread stuffing spilling out on the platter. Just as he picked up the knife, they heard Minnie clattering down the stairs.

"And this," Silas said, "is my little sister Minnie, who has a tendency to be late for dinner."

"Pleased to meet you," Sarah said as Minnie nodded and slipped into the chair beside Silas. Sarah looked up and found him staring at her. She quickly looked away and focused her attention on his father's deft carving of the chicken.

"White or dark?" Mr. Hibbard said, looking at Sarah.

"I prefer white," she said.

"I prefer white, too," Minnie chimed in.

"Plenty here," her father said. "Silas dotes on the drumsticks and is never likely to share."

Without even glancing across the table, Sarah knew Silas's face was reddening. She hoped hers wasn't. Prayed she'd get through this whole meal without cheeks that often burned and embarrassed her. She watched as Mr. Hibbard added two boiled potatoes and two parsnips on her plate and passed it down. He then filled a plate for Silas's mother and one for Minnie. He gave Silas both drumsticks and, finally, took a slab of dark meat for himself.

When she saw Jane Hibbard start to eat, Sarah picked up her fork, grateful to have something ordinary to do. For several minutes no one said anything and then Silas's mother said, "I do favor a little rhubarb sauce on the side with chicken, but the plants have bloomed, and the stalks were tough as saplings this week."

"Even a lot of sugar can't take care of that, Mrs. Hibbard," Sarah said. "But I like that tartness for sauce or pie."

"Do you cook some?" Jane asked. "Way to a man's heart runs through his stomach, you know."

"My sister and I were taught to cook as soon as we were tall enough to reach the pantry shelf and the stove," Sarah said, hoping she wasn't blushing about the thought of a man's heart. "Mostly simple food. Mostly from what we raise. I have to say, ma'am, I'm very partial to parsnips and wonder how you could store them until this late in the year. We only have them in spring."

"Nothing special," Jane Hibbard said, suddenly giving Sarah a real smile. "We have a dark nook in the root cellar where they don't shrivel in the way of apples."

"Mr. Sherman has quite a flock of chickens," Silas said. "And Sarah's sister's friend is raising some very fancy ones, not to be eaten, I gather."

"Does he eat the fancy eggs or let the hens set on them?"

"Both, I think. Haven't seen his place."

Chickens again, Sarah thought. We talked on and on and on about chickens when Silas had Sunday dinner at my house. She had never liked chickens. They seemed sort of dirty, scratching around on the coop floor and eating what they found. She'd refused to eat an egg until her mother explained that the egg and the excrement – what a word – had their own paths out of the hen. Remembering, she smothered a giggle and caught Silas raising an eyebrow. Quickly, she said, "I'd rather cook chickens than take care of them."

Mr. Hibbard laughed out loud at that and said he felt the same way. And Mrs. Hibbard chimed in to say, "If no one feeds 'em, no one eats 'em." Then she focused on Sarah again and asked, "And do you sew?"

"Yes, ma'am." And feeling a little pressured, Sarah added, "And I drive the tedder and the rake."

"Also, if you are performing an inquisition on my friend here," Silas said, "she's the best hay stomper in the county."

"Better keep dancing," Mr. Hibbard said, giving a little chuckle, "and stay out of hay mows."

"Mr. Hibbard!" Jane Hibbard said, quickly changing the subject to ask, "Anyone for more chicken?"

An hour and a piece of blueberry pie later, Silas and Sarah were back in the buggy. Mrs. Hibbard stood on the porch as they went down the driveway, and as Dolly pulled into the road, they both sighed, looked at each other and laughed. A short way along the narrow road, Silas drew in the reins, and as soon as Dolly stopped, he pulled Sarah close and gently kissed her.

"No moon yet," he said. And Sarah, smiling, put both arms around his neck and gave him a long kiss, finally drawing away and tucking her head into his shoulder. He held her, thinking what a wonder this was, this feeling of what he supposed was love. Had his parents had this? He supposed so, though it didn't show much now. Mebbe he and Sarah could be more like her parents as time went by. They talked more than his did. He felt Sarah shiver and pushed her away to find a tear rolling down each cheek.

"What is it?" he said, alarmed. He'd been thinking the dinner went as well as could be expected with his father and mother. And his mother had certainly taken a shine to Sarah, especially about parsnips of all things.

"Happy," she said and started to sob. "Just happy."

Bewildered, he pulled her close and when her shaking stopped, he gently stroked her back, trying to banish the thought that he'd like to stroke all of her. Scare her to death, he reckoned. Dolly jingled her harness and shuffled her feet in place, so Silas picked up the reins and Sarah sat back on the bench, still sniffling.

"Ma took a liking to you," he said, wondering if she'd missed that.

"What about Mr. Hibbard?" Sarah asked.

"Who knows? But he wasn't mean."

"Is he usually?"

"Can be. When he's been at the drink or his head hurts because of it."

"I was a little afraid of him, but I don't feel nervous about your mother anymore. And I loved the parsnips. Haven't had them since April."

"She's a good cook," Silas said.

"But she put three white things on my plate," Sarah commented.

"What does that mean?"

"My mother says you need carrots or green beans on the plate when you serve chicken and parsnips."

"Ah," Silas said. "Looks good and tastes good. Like you."

Sarah laughed and put her hand on his arm.

"You know, I hope, that touching me may mean stopping Dolly again," Silas said.

"I'll take my chances," she said saucily, thinking she wished he'd do that back stroking again – when she wasn't crying her eyes red.

Dolly broke into a trot and for a couple of miles neither

of them said a word. Sarah kept glancing sideways at Silas, thinking how handsome he was and how strange it was that he should say his father was mean sometimes. She knew all about hard cider and had heard her mother say she never wanted that barrel of sin in the Sherman cellar. The only barrels they had contained apples or apple cider allowed to turn into vinegar for cooking. She turned her head and took a closer look at this young man she wanted to kiss again and again.

He caught her looking and grinned. "Need to tell you I'm about to be twice as busy as a bee," he said. "Took a job a couple days a week at the sawmill near Eastborough."

"Whatever for? Your plate's full now."

"Yep. With green beans on it."

She jabbed him with her elbow.

"Need some real money," Silas explained.

"You in debt?" Sarah asked, aware that her father dreaded that possibility as if it were a plague.

"Not."

"Then what?"

"Going to buy a farm of my own."

Sarah gasped. She barely was able to get out the word why. It seemed outlandish for a man so young to be getting his own place.

"Because I want to marry you," Silas said, pulling Dolly to a halt again. "Weren't all that ready to say that now, but you do ask a passel of questions."

Now Sarah's hands were in her lap, and she was staring at them, her fingers twisting around themselves. She did not move.

"I am in love with you, Sarah Sherman, prob'bly from the first day I saw you crying on a rock. Didn't you know?"

Sarah still did not speak. Did not look up. Silas reached for the twisting fingers and cupped them in his big hands until they stopped moving. Then he turned Sarah toward him, putting one hand under her chin and lifting so he could see past the rim of her bonnet. To his dismay, tears were running down her cheeks. Again. He'd been too sudden, she needed more time, maybe she didn't love him.

But Sarah reached for him and kissed him, her tears now running toward his chin. It was a long kiss, and when she pulled away, she stammered, "I wasn't sure, I've never felt like this before, I didn't know what to expect, I hoped …" Her voice trailed off. Silas reached in his pocket and produced a white handkerchief and started to wipe her face.

"What," he asked gently, but a little uncertainly, "were you hoping?"

"That by this time next year, you'd propose and we'd get married and move out of our parents' houses," she said, a small smile appearing as he ran the handkerchief over his own cheeks. "And I would iron your handkerchiefs."

That last made Silas laugh. He jumped down from the seat and asked her to join him on the ground. She stepped down, and he immediately went down on one knee in front of her, took her hands again and blurted, "I am an awkward fool, but I have been a little beside myself ever since I first laid eyes on you, and I am going to try to get this right this time. Will you, Sarah Sherman, marry me?"

"You'd better get up, sir, or you'll ruin your trousers," she said. "And yes, yes, yes. When?"

He couldn't help looking down at his Sunday-go-to-meeting pants as he jumped up and put his arms around her. They stood there, tight together, not speaking until Dolly jingled her harness again.

"Have to wait a bit," he said hesitantly. "Best I get some cash money put aside first or you'll be a bride with no breakfast."

He'd come in from the barn, and she'd have it ready, Sarah thought. And mebbe they'd chat about the weather and what their day would be, and at the end of that day, they'd go to bed and ... she felt a shiver go right down her spine. She didn't know a lot about the going to bed, but it was exciting, especially since nobody talked about it.

"Cold?" Silas asked, still holding her tight, wanting to let his hands wander.

"No, sir, just thinking about being in our own house and not watching you drive away in your buggy. But can we still drive through the bridge? And can we have stenciled walls? And a snow apple tree? And do I have to call you Mr. Hibbard?"

Silas dropped his arms and took her face in his calloused hands. His kiss lasted a long time, and Sarah was startled to feel his tongue against her lips, as if he were trying to open her mouth. Then her lips parted, and she was surprised to find her tongue looking for his and a whole new thrill rippled all the way to her toes. His hands slid down her back, and in spite of layers and layers of clothing, she felt him pull her so tight she could feel a pulsing of what she privately called the "scary part." Then her brain was no longer in charge, and she put her arms around his neck and gave in to her feelings.

"I'd better set you back in the wagon," Silas said, breaking away, his voice strangely hoarse. As he reached to lift her up, his thumbs slid across the roundness of her breasts and, after a few seconds, he abruptly dropped his hands and backed off.

"Sorry. I'm so sorry," Silas said.

Sarah, who had nearly stopped breathing at his touch, managed only a quick, "It's all right." Then she laughed and added, "I liked it, even if I am not supposed to." That made him chuckle and tell her they'd better be getting on before search parties were sent out. Carefully, he lifted her to the seat, still thinking about how wonderful she felt and how it made him feel, despite a lot of layers of fabric.

Back in the buggy, Silas said, "We don't need a bridge, Sarah. But we can go there every Saturday night if it pleases you. And stencils, too, whatever that means. Any apple tree that suits you. And why in God's name would you call me Mr. Hibbard?"

"Like your mother," she said.

"You are almost as funny as Nell sometimes. It's Silas, ma'am, or hey you. I'll answer."

"And you? What do you want?"

"Pleased with whatever joins us together." He leaned toward her and gently kissed her cheek. "From stomping hay to sharing a bed."

She felt the red coming and dropped her head. Bed, there it was again. Frightening. But she could not remember ever being so happy. Within minutes, she slid into a shallow doze, lulled by the steady rhythm of Dolly's gait. Silas glanced at her, watched her lids flicker and then drop and decided Sunday dinner was a considerable success.

John Sherman was coming out of the barn when the buggy pulled into the yard, and he felt a twinge of resentment when he saw his daughter's head on Silas's shoulder. Was he about to lose a daughter? Then he mentally chided himself. He had certainly seen this coming. Sarah hadn't heard half the talk in the house for several weeks because she was inside her own mind most of the time. Lovesick, people called it. He'd never thought love was an ailment, but he knew she was sometimes moving around like a sleepwalker. He liked this young man, he admitted, so he'd give it his blessing. He was quite certain that was coming, perhaps right now. He saw Silas nudge Sarah, who sat up quickly, looked around and waved. He waved back, unable to suppress a grin because he figured they figured they had a secret.

Silas helped Sarah down and whispered, "Should I speak to your father now? Are you ready?"

"Been ready since the first handkerchief," Sarah said, laughing. So she headed for the kitchen door while Silas, feeling as if each of his feet weighed as much as a newborn calf, approached Sarah's father.

"Good trip?" John Sherman said, wondering if the boy would be able to open his mouth and get any words out.

But Silas surprised him. "It could not have been better, sir," he said, without a trace of a stammer but keeping his shaking hands behind his back. "I wish to marry your daughter, and …" Before he could finish, Sarah's father said, "Which one?"

Now Silas was surprised, and in his present state of mind, it took him a second to realize the man was funning him. "Sarah, of course. And I've done it all backwards because I've already asked her, sir, and she said yes and …"

John Sherman interrupted again. "Emma and I saw this coming. Nothing like a long buggy ride to make a man decide things. You certainly have our blessing, but we will need to talk about whether you have the wherewithal to support her."

"Going to work at the sawmill and get a little nest egg going," Silas said. "Hanker to buy a farm of my own soon's I can."

Sarah's father reached out to shake Silas's hand. "Reckon we're going to have a wedding. Son."

Silas was startled to be called son and felt a little guilty for wishing his father called him that – and never had. He tied Dolly to the hitching post by the path and the two headed for the house, where they found Emma hugging Sarah.

"I spilled the beans," Sarah said. "I couldn't wait."

"What made you think I'd give consent?" her father growled.

"How could you not?" Sarah said, instantly thinking she'd been impertinent. "Sir."

"Couldn't," he admitted, laughing. "And your young man now needs to be on his way. He won't be home till after dark as it is."

"Dolly knows the road," Silas said. "She'll get me home." So he shook hands with Sarah's father again and was surprised when her mother gave him a peck on the cheek. He and Sarah walked out to the buggy and stood, arms around each other, each stunned by the warmth of the other, each wondering if it was the same for the other. Then he pushed her bonnet back, kissed the top of her head, jumped into the buggy seat, spoke to Dolly and quickly rattled down the gravel driveway. She watched until he rounded the turn by the giant oak tree and was out of sight. She hoped her father and mother hadn't been watching but reckoned that was a wish in vain.

CHAPTER TWELVE

A FEW DAYS later, at the second to last farm on Apple Road, Jason fed his chickens, milked the cows and then sat on the split rails of the pasture gate to watch the sun go down. She was pretty, that Nell, he thought, and feisty. He couldn't remember when anyone had made him laugh as much as she did, and it startled him to realize he could recall her very words, one time and another – and another. Never even listened much to womenfolk talking before. Now he was surprised at how much more he wanted to hear. He watched as a flock of crows settled into his small cornfield and figured he'd start the music tomorrow to keep them away from the late harvest. Only take ten minutes to hang the wood scraps he'd saved and strung together so they'd rattle in the breeze. And rattle the crows, he hoped. The neighbors laughed at his attempt to trick nature, but his corn crop would be bigger than theirs.

 He scraped his boots on the lower rail and started thinking about Nell again. His mother would call her a flirt, and he reckoned that was right. But he liked it when she flirted with him. And he liked even more the way she kissed him and traced the curves of his ears with her fingers. He'd walked out with a few girls over the past couple of years, but none like Nell. Nobody who'd touched his ears, he thought with a chuckle. Never thought about them before that, except when they tingled with cold in January. As the sun dipped behind a long strip of gray clouds, he let his mind see her in his kitchen, his workshop, his chicken house. Suddenly, he slapped himself on the side of the head and said aloud, "What the devil are you thinking, Jason? You want to get married?" He jumped down from the gate and started pacing up and down along the fence. It was his custom about this time of day to figure out what had to be done tomorrow. But the Nell thoughts smothered work ideas, and he found himself going back to the picture of her in his kitchen, cooking oats and baking beans. As he reached the house, he let out a loud whoop. She might suggest he go fly a kite, but he was going to find out. Waiting might mean being in the back row when she was up front tying the knot with some other farmer. Thing to do was ask her father if he could come around. That had worked right well for Silas.

    He woke before the sun the next morning, the rumpled sheet damp with humidity that had never gone to its bed. In his kitchen, he poked up the fire in the stove and warmed a small spider. Watching the butter sputter in the pan, he thought of Nell again and what a pleasant morning a man would have if breakfast was hot and ready when first chores were done. He cracked two eggs, one white-shelled and the other green, into the hot butter. It would, he admitted, be an even more pleasant day if he'd shared his bed with a woman. His bed – that was worth thinking about. Not any woman, he was beginning to think. Nell Sherman. He grinned thinking how saucy she was, especially compared to her sister. Demure, that was the word for Sarah.

Eating quickly, he fed his chickens, milked cows, did a half-baked – could she bake, he wondered – job of mucking the barn and promised himself to finish it later. He was due by seven at the Clark sawmill where he put in a few hours a week in return for choice pieces of lumber for his furniture. He heard the whine of the saws before the mill was in sight, and as he turned the last corner was startled to find Silas dismounting his horse and looking around the yard for a place to tie her.

"What in tarnation are you doing here," Jason demanded. "Every time I turn around, you are there."

"I might ask you the same," Silas said, laughing. "Had a need of a cash job to get enough to put money down on a farm."

"Your own farm?"

"Yep."

"You fixin' to get married to Sarah Sherman?"

Silas looked puzzled and muttered, "Word does get around."

"I was just putting three and three together," Jason said, grinning. "Pretty plain you were mooning over her and can't say as I blame you. But pretty sudden?"

"You've been doing a little mooning yourself," Silas said, a little annoyed at the question.

"Truth is," Jason said hesitantly, "I do fancy her sister. Have her on my mind."

At that, Silas grinned and offered his hand. They shook, and Jason said, "I'll show you around."

Four hours later, sweating and dirty with sawdust, they took their lunch pails and sat down under the nearest tree to eat. Silas felt like his stomach had a hole in it. Well, he supposed it did, probably two. One for in, one for out. But right now it was hollow. He hoped his ma had put in a piece of her apple pie, and there it was. He ate it first and then took out the thick chunks of brown bread. He glanced at Jason's food and saw he was peeling a blue egg. Well, the egg wasn't blue but the shell was. "That from a special chicken?" he asked.

"Ayuh. Tastes just the same as any old egg. Whatcha think of your new profession?"

"Tough stuff. Bit put off by the big saw."

"Stay scared. I don't want a brother-in-law with a stump for a thumb."

"Did you already ask her?" Silas asked in surprise.

"Nope. Best I ask her father first, right?"

"I did," Silas said. "Lot easier than I thought it would be. Can't imagine anyone asking my pa if he could call on my sister. He'd prob'bly say yes in the end, but not before he roared around for some time. You serious?"

"Reckon so. Gettin' more certain by the day."

The mill bell rang, and they jumped up, gathered up the leavings of the noon meal and headed back to work. When the day was done, they wrote down their time in the ledger and headed home. As Silas trotted past Jason on Dolly, he called, "See him now. You're so dirty he'll know you're a hard worker and might provide for his daughter."

"You back here tomorrow?" Jason asked, looking down at his filthy pants and boots turned pale with sawdust.

"Nobody fired me yet," Silas said.

"I'm done till next week. You watch yourself with that saw."

Cantering home, Silas thought about how he'd tell his parents. He knew his mother thought something was up, and he reckoned he'd tell her first. When he reached the farm, he put Dolly in her stall, rubbed her down and put grain in her bin. He walked to the house slowly, brushing off sawdust as he went, thinking how to go about this. He knew very well that the money he brought in with his deliveries made ends meet. Married, he'd be leaving them on their own. His mother opened the door before he reached it and said, "Better get out of those pants right there, or I'll be sweeping through Wednesday. Can't figure why you took on such a dirty job." So he stopped on the steps to shed shoes and pants and give both a good shake, relieved that she'd given him an opening.

She had already gone back to cutting the ends off wax beans, but she dropped the knife when he said, "Pay isn't bad, Ma, and I'm saving to put something down on a farm of my own."

"Getting hitched?" she asked. "Reckoned something was up with that Sarah Sherman."

"Soon's I'm ready," Silas answered, startled and not sure how his mother was taking this.

"Seems like a fine young woman," she said, and went back to cutting beans. Silas waited, and when his mother put the beans on the stove, he asked, "What do you think about the farm?"

"It's high time you moved along, Silas. Not certain what happens here when you go, don't know one day to the next what's around the corner. Your pa bears watching when it comes to seeing to things." She stared out the window and said almost to herself, "Never know when a frog may seek a bigger pond." Then she smiled and added, "I have a high opinion of that young woman."

Silas wanted to give her a hug but refrained. Too often in the past, she'd said, "Don't need any of that sass," when faced with affection. So he patted her shoulder and headed upstairs to change out of his dusty clothes. A bath would be grand, but it wasn't Saturday. He pulled off all his work clothes and wondered what that frog and pond business was all about. But he'd learned from Sarah that women's minds did not travel in straight lines.

At his house, Jason pondered Silas's words. Chores finished, he shed his clothes and walked into the small pond behind the barn. He didn't have any soap, but he could get rid of the sawdust. He went under and came up in the midst of a considerable amount of floating sawdust. He jumped out, grabbed his clothes and ran for the house, knowing no one was about but not wanting to risk town gossip about his cavorting about naked as a newborn. Upstairs, he put on a clean shirt and trousers and went back to the barn. He'd ride over to the Sherman place now and see Nell's father. He gritted his teeth and admitted he hadn't been this scared since he'd faced a really smart girl in the finals of his last school spelling bee. Well, he recalled, he'd won that, hadn't he. With "brougham." She'd spelled "broom," and it was done. He knew about those new-fangled buggies.

As he rode up to the Sherman place, he noticed all the rockers on the porch were filled. More than the family, he reckoned. Leastways, he wouldn't be interrupting supper.

But he'd have to figure a way to get Nell out of the crowd. To his relief, he saw her get up and come down the steps just as he reached the house.

"Did you come for the ice cream?" she said.

"What?"

"Couple of cousins from Vermont jes' plain dropped in, no notice, so we're all settin' out here taking turns with the crank. Father let us have enough ice for one batch, and it'll be ready in another hour or thereabouts. Hopin' the neighbors who appeared out of nowhere won't eat much," she whispered.

"Are you next for the crank, or can you spare a half hour? Nice evening for a little walk before ice cream."

"I've time, long's I get back for my turn and my bowlful," Nell answered. "Where'd you want to go?"

"Out of sight of the ice cream makers, I reckon."

Nell felt herself blushing, but she linked her arm through his, waved to the porch and walked toward the barn. Once out of sight, she stopped and faced him. "Rather perch on the gate than walk. Long day in the field today, and my feet don't want to pick up and put down much more."

"Long day in the sawdust for me," Jason said. He headed for the fence and boosted her onto the top rail, keeping his hands tight on her waist. Instead of joining her, he looked up and said, "I'd like to think about you making ice cream at my house."

"Why on earth …" She stopped abruptly when she saw his face.

"Marry me, Nell," he said. "I want you in my house, in my barn, in my bed, with or without ice cream."

Nell started to laugh, and his heart sank. He looked down at his shoes, wondering what in tarnation had made him think this beautiful girl would accept the likes of him. She was still laughing when she said, "That's the dangdest proposal any girl ever got, and I was beginning to fret that I might have to ask you." And she jumped down into his arms and kissed him on the mouth, pulling away just long enough to say, "yes, yes, yes" and then kissing him again. Jason held her close, burying his head in her hair, feeling his anxiety over this moment slide away and exhilaration grow, as he pulled the whole length of her tight against him. She put her arms around his neck, and when she stretched up, he could feel her breasts against his thin shirt. She lifted his head and kissed him again, her fingers tracing the curves of his ears. As one, they shivered, and she broke away.

"Shivering, and we haven't even had the ice cream," she said, laughing again. She didn't quite know what to do next, and that was a new sensation for her. She'd always just jumped into whatever was happening, usually without thinking.

Jason wasn't thinking too clearly, either, but he reckoned they'd better get back in sight of the group or he'd be wishing he was in the haymow with this girl. His girl. He liked that. In his impatience, he'd gone and put the buggy in front of the horse, and he needed to ask her father. Would that be before or after ice cream? He didn't know.

Taking both of her hands, he said, "Do I speak to your father now?"

"After the ice cream," she said, confidently. "Besides, I think he already knows. He knows so many things before they happen."

"Time for you to crank, I'll wager," he said, and they walked quickly, holding hands, toward the house and the waiting dessert.

When Sarah watched them walk oh, so slowly up the path, she told herself they were going to get married, too. Had he asked her? She'd wager her best petticoat on it. And weren't they the bold ones, plighting their troth before he'd asked Father for her hand. Good thing you didn't have to actually give the hand, she thought, and giggled at the grisly idea. It'd be a poor wife who'd be trying to handle her chores without two hands. There I go, she thought, letting my brain spatter everywhere – hadn't she just put stenciled walls and kissing on a bridge in the same sentence?

Then they were on the porch, and Jason, anxious to get this duty done, edged toward John Sherman, leaned in and muttered something she couldn't hear. Both men stepped off the porch, and Sarah saw that Nell was cranking away, head down, listening intently, but not looking. Clever, Sarah thought. Nell rocked slowly, smiling, then looked up to see her mother watching her. Emma looked away, but Sarah saw her mother's attention move to the spot a hundred feet away where her father and Jason were talking. She could see Jason's mouth moving and realized he was staring at something in the distance while Father was watching him closely. Then Jason stopped talking and stood, hands behind his back, one boot toe tracing a circle in the gravel. She saw her father's lips move, glanced back at her mother and saw that she was focused on the pair as well. Then John Sherman thrust his hand out, and Jason grabbed it, a wide smile on his face.

Walking back to the group, Jason felt as uneasy as a boy who needs the privy at school and doesn't want to ask. But he should have spared himself. The two were several feet away from the ice cream makers when John Sherman's big voice boomed, "Seems, Emma, we're going to marry off our daughters all to onc't." That made Sarah jump up and grab Nell, who was turning as red as a ripe tomato, twirling her around with reckless disregard of the ice cream tub, saying, "You knew, didn't you. You didn't tell, but he asked you before he ever spoke with Father."

Eyes shining, Nell grinned and said, "Did. Now let go of me." Sarah did one last twirl, and Nell dropped to her knees and went back to the task of cranking the ice cream. But Jason's anxiety had vanished, and he went straight to Nell and to the delight of everyone on the porch, knelt beside her, took the wooden handle away from her and proceeded to make ice cream. It took only a few more minutes when Emma peeked in, pronounced it ready and set out the bowls and spoons. While they lined up, Jason grabbed Nell's hand.

"Let's get in line," she said, still pink but grinning at him. He shook his head, pulled her toward the end of the line and quietly turned her toward the house. He was certain at least Sarah had taken notice of the move, so he kept walking until they were out of sight of the windows. Then he turned, put his arms around Nell and held her so tight that she gave a small gasp. So he released her and said, "Needed to kiss my girl, my Nell, right now."

So he did, long and soft and so sweet that Nell thought she might just slip to the floor, melted like butter in the sun. She steadied herself by grabbing his shirt, and when he stopped, she reached up and kissed him back, long but not soft, and for the first time, she let her lips part when she felt his tongue. Briefly, she wondered if Sarah had done this with Silas, and then she opened her mouth and was lost in the moment. But the moment was short. Jason heard a door open somewhere behind them and said, "We have to go back."

"That," Nell said, trying to get back her usual sauciness, "that ..." Her voice trailed off, and she was overwhelmed by the idea that she, for perhaps the first time in her life, was speechless.

Jason's hand on her arm tightened and he whispered, "That, ice cream girl, is only the beginning." So, still feeling a little wobbly, Nell managed a laugh, and they went back to the porch to smiles and hugs all around. And when it was time for the sisters to embrace, Nell whispered, "Oh, my." And Sarah nodded.

CHAPTER THIRTEEN

"'Bout to lose all my daughters," John Sherman said as soon as they sat down to supper the next day.

"You already said that, Father," Nell said.

"And it was true," Emma chimed in. "I am a bit fussed already about hope chests and wedding clothing and cooking supper for only two."

Nell and Sarah exchanged glances and nods, and Sarah said, "We're not getting married tomorrow, Father. Silas is working the sawmill and putting money aside to get a farm of his own."

"And what about you, Nell?" Emma asked.

"Jason hasn't said anything about time, and he already has a place of his own, well, a place that he rents, and he wants me there making ice cream and …" She paused, realizing that she wouldn't mention he wanted to share a bed, and then went on, "Perhaps soon?"

Sarah clapped her hands and cried, "We could both get married at the same time, and we could live with you and Jason, Nell, until Silas has his farm, or we could live here, Father, so you could ease into losing us, or we could live with Silas's parents." She stopped and added, "Well, mebbe not that last. I am not certain Silas's father thinks I'm a good thing."

"How could he not?" John said testily. "You cook, you sew, you hay, you have a high school diploma. Does he?"

"Does he what?" Sarah said, taken aback by the outburst.
"Have a high school diploma," her father answered.
"I have no idea, but I'm not marrying Mr. Hibbard. And Silas does, if that matters. Sir."
"I'd like to do that," Nell said.
"Do what?" Emma asked, totally confounded by this conversation.
"Get married together. And surely Jason can wait a bit to enjoy all my talents. And I hope you won't be offended, Sarah, but I'm ready to not live with you." That made Sarah laugh, and then the two hugged again, laughing and crying.

A little earlier and a few miles away, Silas had dozed on his horse, reins loose in his hands, exhausted from the day at the sawmill. Dolly, not yet familiar with this run, trotted on as if he were wide awake and somehow managed to get him home at dusk. He roused when she came to a halt at the barn door and was surprised to see a dim light inside the house. His parents often sat in darkness or went to bed early, and he'd often thought both behaviors were related to what he considered their infernal need to save. Now, thinking about marrying Sarah, his irritation with his parents' frugal ways ebbed. Wasn't he saving every penny himself? He stored Dolly's harness, gave her grain and water and a pat on the flank and headed for the house, hoping to find a bit of supper.

He found his parents at the kitchen table, poring over several sheets of paper that seemed to be covered with numbers. When his father greeted him with a smile, he realized that for once there'd been no visits to the keg in the cellar. He was clear-eyed. His skin wasn't flushed with hard-cider heat. Silas pulled out a chair and sat down, looking at the figures curiously.

"Buying a new place, Silas," Caleb Hibbard said.

"That so?" Silas said, trying to sound as if it were quite ordinary news.

"In Eastborough," Jane Hibbard added. "Time and tide wait for no man, so we're in a bit of a hurry here."

"But figuring, Silas, doing the figuring," his father added. "P'raps, with your high schooling, you could make somethin' of it." He pushed one of the papers across the table, and Silas glanced around the room at the scratched table, the blackened kettle on the stove, the raveled hand towel by the sink. For the first time, he realized his parents, while he had considered them parsimonious, even stingy, might have been putting away a few dollars for quite a long time. They'd need a mortgage, but it wouldn't be a burden, if things went right.

"Not bad," he said, cautiously, after letting the figures slide through his head and organize themselves. He hoped he was really being asked for his opinion. "Where's the place?"

"Eastborough. Up on a hill above town," Jane said. "Family named Alden has owned it for years. We heard at Grange that Jed Alden had died, and Mary would not stay on."

"Eastborough? Grange?" Silas asked.

"Last month's meeting," his father said. "Your ma was anxious to speak for it, and we done just that."

"Nothing ventured, nothing gained," Jane Hibbard said. "Something big to take on just as you seem on the brink of a new life. Reckon we need to know your intentions about that young woman who seems to have you walking around like a blindfolded cat these days."

"Lot coming at once here," Silas said, trying to speak in a normal tone.

"Ay-ah," his mother answered. "Life. It never rains but it pours."

Silas started to laugh, amused not for the first time at the way worn, old sayings tumbled from his mother's mouth so naturally. He answered, "Seems more like make hay when the sun shines to me."

"Don't be funning me, young man," his mother snapped. But she smiled as she spoke. "Not letting you off, Silas. Will she have you?"

"Yes."

Silas's father chuckled. "You could say, Mrs. Hibbard, he's a chip off the old block, if you were a-mind to. Always telling me I don't say enough, don't bring home the gossip. He's answered. I reckon the next question is 'When'?"

"Soon's I have enough saved to put cash down on a place of my own," Silas said with a sigh. "Not too long, I'm hopin'."

"Be right nice to have you around to help with the new place," Jane Hibbard said. "But we aren't going to stand in the way of a new life with the Sherman girl. We was, believe it or not, young onc't."

His eyes still on the papers in front of him, Caleb Hibbard said almost in a whisper, "Could pr'aps figure a way give your new life and your new wife a place on the farm until you were ready to get your own place. Couple more years before Minnie will be big enough to lend a hand."

"Have to talk to Sarah about that," Silas said, not letting his face show how much he would like the idea. They'd be able to marry that much sooner, he thought. And said to his mother, "Appreciate if you call her Sarah. 'The Sherman girl' sounds right unfriendly."

"Sarah it is. You think on it and let Mr. Hibbard know soon. Reckon we'll take the chance and sign the papers as soon as we can get to the bank." To Silas's surprise, she actually chuckled as she said, "The die is cast." Silas chuckled, too, thinking he'd paid no mind till this day to the Mr. Hibbard thing.

"What, Ma, do you know about stencils on walls?" he asked.

"I know you're changing horses in midstream here, and I know stencils are painted on and are right pretty. Put right on the plaster. Why?"

"Sarah has a hankering for stenciled walls," he said. "And I've never seen such."

"Hiring that out might be dear. Most folks prob'bly do it theirselves."

"Says she's a good hay stomper, but don't know if that qualifies for painting," Silas said, laughing. But a quick study on kisses, he thought. He pushed that memory aside and said, "Hope to be married in a year or so."

"Ay-uh," his mother said. "Don't know if your pa will be much on weddings, but I'd like to be there. If invited."

"No question. At the church in Eastborough, I reckon, but that's all up to Sarah. I'll just be there. Any supper left?"

CHAPTER FOURTEEN

Sarah sat down at the table and felt as if lightning had leapt into the room. It was usually a quiet meal, but yesterday's news had everyone bubbling over. She looked across the table at Nell and started to giggle. Then they were both giggling, which made John Sherman smile. Both married, he thought. Going to cost me a pretty penny, but two-for-one – that's a blessing. He looked down the table at Emma and saw she had a tear in her eye but was smiling, too.

"Pleased as punch for both of you," he said. "A fine pair of young men. A little worried that one of you found a beau by crying at a fair and the other by grabbing a hand at a square dance. Not the usual courting. But neither of you has been prone to the ordinary." He tilted his chair back, saw Emma frown, and set four legs on the floor again. "How in tarnation does a father walk two brides down the aisle?"

"Both at once," Nell said quickly.

"One at a time," Sarah said. And then the sisters started to giggle again.

"We will put our minds on it," Emma said. "But there will be no quarreling. Just deciding."

Both girls nodded and went back to eating, occasionally looking up from their bowls of soup to grin at each other, their excitement running like a current through the room. The meal finished, they all tucked their napkins into the silver rings that Emma treasured, and the sisters cleared. They laughed at the startled look on their father's face when their mother announced that she and John would be taking a walk while the girls washed up. But John Sherman didn't question. He put aside his habit of napping at the table and stood, offering his arm to Emma. Through the kitchen window, the sisters watched their parents walk down the path and out of sight.

"Whatever for?" Nell wondered.

"Something about us," Sarah said, having no idea what was being discussed out of their hearing.

"And what will we wear?" Nell said, losing interest in whatever the secret conversation might concern.

"Lace and a passel of buttons and buttonholes to sew," Sarah sighed. "And I don't want to go down the aisle with you. Just as soon wait down front, in truth."

"Well, you can't," Nell retorted. "And I've changed my mind about both at once anyway. You'll look much prettier than I will."

"Nell! Why do you say that? I'll look like a scared rabbit. Alice's white rabbit. Hoping to find the hole."

"Because it's true. You've always been prettier. And you can't get married in a hole." That set them to giggling again, but when they stopped, Sarah went back to the talk about the aisle in the church.

"And you'll march that aisle as if you've done it a dozen times, looking as if it were a piece of cake. And I'll be as red as a cooked beet, tripping on my dress."

"Who will make the cake?" Nell asked, instantly onto a

new topic, in her usual impulsive way. "We'll need a cake," adding, "you are a silly goose."

"And sheets and blankets and dishware and new nightdresses," Sarah said, also making a leap.

"You may hold back in a crowd, Sarah, but you're always the sensible one. Some girls start their hope chests when they're fourteen, but we didn't." She paused and said, thoughtfully, "which doesn't mean Mother didn't do exactly that."

"Where would she keep such?" Sarah asked, drying the last bowl and stacking it in the cupboard.

"How long do you think they'll be walking?" Nell asked, hoping they had time to hunt for a hope chest, or two of them.

"She has a large trunk in the attic," Sarah offered.

"Let's go!"

So the two ran up the attic stairs and found a trunk behind a couple of chairs with only three legs. Nell watched out the tiny attic window while Sarah tried to unlatch the trunk, but it was locked.

"Can't open it," she said.

"And we need to skedaddle downstairs. They're coming back."

Holding up their long skirts, they rushed down the narrow attic stairs and were seated in the parlor when John and Emma came in and sat down. Neither was smiling, and the sisters saw that their father was twiddling his thumbs, which always meant some announcement was coming. But it was Emma who spoke.

"Taffeta," she said. "We will make dresses in taffeta."

"Mother?" Nell said anxiously. "What does that mean?"

"Means it would be foolish to spend hours sewing dresses that can never be worn again."

"What your mother is saying, girls," John Sherman said, "is that we will have two fine weddings on the same day with an ice cream social or some such after the church ceremony, and we will do it well but not extravagantly. And we are hoping you are agreeable."

"Yes!" Sarah said, relieved that they still approved of her marrying Silas.

"Yes, but not plaid," Nell said, always a little unwilling to instantly agree with anything.

"I'm partial to stripes," Emma said, "with wide lace cuffs and lace at the throat, both of which could be removed after the ceremony."

"And we'd end up with a 'best dress,'" Sarah said, nodding and wishing Nell would not throw up any stone walls. "We'll need a year to make such, I reckon."

Emma nodded. "I think a full skirt attached to a bodice that cuts into the skirt with a V. I will have to get to Ripton to see the fabrics for myself."

Sarah was excited about telling Silas about all this, but Nell wanted to know if they could accompany her on the fabric trip. Emma hesitated only a second before nodding.

"So it's settled," John said. "Time for chores." And he headed to the back room to pull on his overalls over his Sunday trousers and exchange shoes for barn boots. In the dining room, Emma sighed and said, "Mebbe I should just be grateful that he's leaving it to me. Makes one less carrot in the stew."

"I have to start a hope chest," Nell and Sarah said in unison. "Not a lot of time," Nell added.

"I've made a little provision for that kind of thing," Emma said, the lines on her sun-worn face outlined by a smile. "And you girls will have to set to and make many more things."

"Can we see?" Nell asked, sounding like a child at the penny candy counter. "Can we see?"

"Indeed. And we'll wait until tomorrow," Emma said firmly. "Now, what about Minnie? You can each attend the other one at the wedding, but I'm given to understand that Silas has a little sister."

"Flower girl," Sarah said immediately. "She can carry flowers and herbs in a basket and walk in front of me. Then everyone will look at her. And how did you know he had a sister?"

"You have to ask questions here and there when your girls start sashaying around with handsome young men," Emma said.

"You gossiped about us," Nell cried. "And I know nothing about Jason except chickens and tables."

"You'll learn soon enough," Emma said. "For better or for worse, as they say."

"What does *that* mean?"

"He's lived alone for some time," Emma said. "Likely a little set in his ways. Sometimes men have to be taught a few things."

"Like what?" Nell said. And then, quietly, "Please tell."

"Like not tramping in from the barn to a clean kitchen floor," her mother said a bit crisply.

"Seems simple enough," Nell muttered. "I'll just tell him."

A small smile was all she received from her mother.

"What about Silas?" Sarah wanted to know.

"Been living at home, so it's likely he doesn't traipse through the house in barn boots or leave his dirty socks on the floor."

"Oh, my," Nell said and scowled at Sarah, who couldn't keep down a giggle.

Everyone went to bed early that night, but the sisters couldn't stop talking about taffeta gowns and flowers and what was in the trunk in the attic. Nell wanted to light a candle and go up there, soon as they heard their father snoring. But Sarah was worried they'd drop the candle and set the house on fire.

"You are such a chicken," Nell grumbled.

"How often have we done something sneaky and been caught?" Sarah demanded, her voice rising.

"Time to pipe down in there," came Emma's voice. Nell quietly tossed the blanket back and tiptoed across the room, avoiding the board that creaked. She pushed the door closed but didn't click the latch.

"Jason," Nell began, whispering as she crawled back into bed, "said he wants me in his bed." Her voice uncharacteristically shaky, she added, "What does that mean – exactly?"

"Exactly, I don't know," Sarah whispered, surprised at the uncertain tone in Nell's question. She was always so sure of everything. "But I know bulls climb on cows' backs, and roosters attack hens, and then we get calves and chickens."

"And that should make me feel good?" Nell said, but she laughed a little.

SARAH MEETS SILAS

"Should we ask Mother?"

"Let's just ask her about the trunk," Nell said, turning over and closing her eyes. In minutes, both were asleep, Nell tossing about as roosters perched on bedsteads and crowed in her dreams. Beside her, barely moving, Sarah dreamed of yards and yards of striped taffeta whipping through the slats of a covered bridge and wrapping around Silas's face.

On her side of her spool bed, Emma lay awake for a long time. Two daughters gone all at once. It was hard. Her babies grown and gone to their own houses. Their empty beds here. What would John do about all the farm work without them? She had dreamed sometimes about the girls marrying professionals and getting away from the hardscrabble days of farming. Still, she knew she had prepared both for the wifely ways of a farmer's spouse, from house to barn to field. At least Jason had the furniture business, but did it amount to much? And on short acquaintance, she sensed that Jason Harris admired Nell's saucy spirit and would let it live. Sarah was so different, so much sweeter, so quick to be hurt, and Silas seemed attuned to that. She could only hope, even as she remembered Sarah saying Silas's father was "sometimes mean." What did "mean" mean?

Beside her, John stirred and she felt his hand on her hip. She pushed closer to him, thinking he might at times be stern, but never mean. She heard herself whisper out loud, "Things work out. And dawn is coming." And she drifted off to the rhythmic sound of his soft snores.

In Grafton, Silas tossed and turned, caught between the joy of owning a place of his own, his and Sarah's, and a niggling worry that he wouldn't be up to snuff as a husband. Be nice to start off in our own place, he thought, but he reckoned neither of them wanted to wait. It'd give him time to get some more cash laid by. For stenciled walls. He smiled, staring at the plain walls of his room. If she was given to painting, he'd let her practice here – or at his folks' new place. He did love to hear her talk, her mind jumping around like a grasshopper. His parents talked so little. He didn't want to be like that.

ACKNOWLEDGMENTS

IN REAL LIFE, my great-grandmother was Sarah Jane Sherman, and her sewing rocker, cane seat and back, redone by my mother, stands in the corner of my bedroom. That's basically all I know about her, except that her formal photograph shows a weathered face, a severe hairstyle and a mouth set in a straight line. Perhaps the hardscrabble life of a New England farm wife created that face – or perhaps it was the anxiety of facing a photographer and the need to sit still for the long exposure time required by the camera. But as a writer, I could make the young Sarah into whomever I wanted her to be – and so I did.

I am indebted to my father's accounts of his early life for the few things I know about my grandmother's childhood: that she went to school at the age of three, that she lost her mother in her early teens, that she had to take over the household and deal with a grieving father who became addicted to hard cider. The original "Sarah's Daughter" filled in all the blanks as I fictionalized my grandmother. I also owe thanks to my Bates College classmate Dave Wyllie who challenged me to write this prequel by asking why Sarah married Silas in the first place. The question stayed in my head and eventually moved into my fingers.

As always, deep thanks go to Cia Elkin, who has edited all of the "Sarah" books and whose skill, thoughtful support and friendship are treasured. Cia's enthusiasm about meeting an earlier generation of the Sherman/Hibbard families gave me confidence about the idea of a prequel. And, as always, author and poet and friend Judy Viorst helped me believe that my characters' lives mattered, their problems and joys believable.

It is wonderful to have granddaughter and graphic designer Summer Wojtas design the cover of "Sarah Meets Silas," as she did for "A Silver Moon for Rose" and the e-book for "Rose." Summer patiently dealt with my second, third and fourth thoughts and showed her expertise in incorporating them or defending her ideas.

Appreciation also goes to Larry Gadd for advice and help on a couple of fronts, the experts at Troy Book Makers who eased the way in the knotty business of publication – and to the friends and strangers who have sent emails and snail mails about their enjoyment of the trilogy about Sarah and Rose.

About the Author

As a newspaper reporter, editor and columnist, Ruth Bass has been telling the stories of real people for a long time. A descendant of generations of New Englanders, she has listened all her life – often at family dinner tables – to anecdotes about people very much like the characters in her novels. In addition to the three books about Rose Hibbard, she is author of eight herbal cookbooks and continues to write her weekly column for The Berkshire Eagle.

A resident of the Berkshires for 60 years, she has won many awards for writing and editing and has been inducted into the New England Press Association's Hall of Fame. A graduate of Bates College with a master's in journalism from Columbia University, she also has an honorary doctorate of humane letters from Westfield State University.

With her late husband, theater critic and novelist Milton Bass, she has three adult children and six grandchildren. Her 20 acres of hillside land cater to her interest in flower and vegetable gardening, along with bird watching. She also enjoys golf, knitting, reading, cooking and photography.